Repetition

Also by Alain Robbe-Grillet:

ALAIN ROBBE-GRILLET

Repetition

Translated from the French by Richard Howard

Grove Press
New York

Originally published in the French language by Editions de Minuit, Paris, France.

Published simultaneously in Canada
Printed in the United States of America

FIRST EDITION

Library of Congress Cataloging-in-Publication Data
Robbe-Grillet, Alain, 1922–
[Reprise. English]
Repetition : a novel / by Alain Robbe-Grillet ; translated from the French by Richard Howard.
p. cm.
ISBN 0-8021-1736-8
I. Howard, Richard, 1929–   II. Title.
PQ2635.O117R4813 2003
843'.914—dc21   2002035448

Grove Press
841 Broadway
New York, NY 10003

03 04 05 06 07   10 9 8 7 6 5 4 3 2 1

Repetition and recollection are the same movement, only in opposite directions, for what is recollected has been: it is repeated backward, whereas repetition properly so-called is recollected forward.

SØREN KIERKEGAARD, *Repetition*

And I don't want to be bothered with eternal complaints about inexact or contradictory details. This report is concerned with objective reality, not with some so-called historical truth.

A. R.-G.

Repetition

Prologue

Here, then, I repeat, and I sum up. During the endless train journey which took me from Eisenach to Berlin across a Thuringia and Saxony in ruins, I noticed, for the first time in I don't know how long, that man whom I call my double, to simplify matters, or else my twin, or again and less theatrically, the traveler.

The train was moving at an uncertain and discontinuous rhythm, making frequent stops, sometimes in the middle of the countryside, obviously because of the state of the tracks, which were still partially unusable or too hastily repaired, but also because of the mysterious and repeated inspections made by the Soviet military government. At one excessively long stop in a sizeable station which must have been Halle-Hauptbahnhof (though I saw no signboard to that effect), I stepped onto the platform to stretch my legs. Most of the station buildings seemed to have been destroyed, as was the entire neighborhood below, sloping to the left.

In the bluish winter daylight, patches of wall several stories high thrust their fragile lacework and their nightmarish silence into the uniformly gray sky. Inexplicably, unless by the persistent effects of an icy morning fog, which must have lasted longer here than elsewhere, the receding planes of these delicate silhouettes shone with the flashy brilliance of something artificial. Like some surrealistic vista (a sort of hole in ordinary space), the entire scene exerts an incomprehensible power of fascination on the mind.

Judging by views down cross-streets, and also in certain limited areas where the buildings are virtually razed to their foundations, it is evident that the main highway has been totally cleared and swept clean, the piles of minor debris doubtless removed by trucks instead of accumulating on the shoulders, just as I remembered seeing them cleared away in Brest, where I was born. Only here and there, breaking the alignment of the ruins, some giant block of masonry is left, like the shaft of a Greek column lying in some archeological dig. All the streets are empty, without a single vehicle or pedestrian. I had no idea the city of Halle had suffered so much from the Anglo-American bombardments, so that now, four years after the armistice, one still sees such huge zones without a sign of reconstruction. Perhaps this isn't Halle after all, but some other big town? I'm

not at all familiar with these parts, having previously reached
Berlin (when, actually, and how many times?) only by the
usual Paris-Warsaw axis—in other words, much farther to
the north. I don't have a map with me, and I can only guess
that the hazards of the rail system have forced us to make a
detour today, after Erfurt and Weimar, as far east as Leipzig
and on another line.

At this moment in my dreamy speculations, the train has
finally started up, without warning, but so slowly, luckily, that
I have had no difficulty returning to my car and climbing back
on. I was then astonished to discover the exceptional length
of the entire train. Had more cars been added? And where
would that have occurred? Like the lifeless city, the platforms
were now completely deserted, as if the last inhabitants had
just managed to embark in order to escape.

In startling contrast, a much denser crowd than at our
arrival in the station now filled the corridor, and I had some
difficulty threading my way between all these human beings
who seemed as overstuffed as their bulging suitcases and
their apparently improvised luggage, shapeless boxes clumsily roped together and blocking the floor of the train. The
stern faces of the men and women, their features drawn with
fatigue, followed me with vaguely reproachful and perhaps
even hostile glances as I struggled past, certainly without
amenity despite my smiles. . . . Unless these wretched people,
apparently in some distress, were merely startled by my
incongruous presence among them, my comfortable clothes,
and the excuses I stammered in schoolboy German as I
passed through emphasizing my foreign status.

Distracted by the additional discomfort I was involuntarily inflicting on them, I passed my compartment without recognizing it, and finding myself at the end of the corridor, I had to turn back toward the front of the train. This time their hitherto mute discontent was expressed by exasperated grumbles and exclamations in a Saxon dialect whose words for the most part escaped me, if not their probable meaning. Having finally caught sight of my thick black dispatch case in the baggage net next to the open compartment door, I managed to identify my seat—my former seat—which was now occupied, as indeed were both banquettes, by several additional children squeezed between their parents or sitting on their laps. And standing against the window was even one more adult, who, when I stepped into the compartment, turned around to give me a close look.

Not certain what to do next, I stood facing the usurper, who was reading a Berlin newspaper spread out in front of his face. No one spoke a word, all eyes—even the children's—converging upon me with unendurable fixity. But no one seemed willing to testify to my right to that seat which I had selected at the start of the trip (Eisenach has become a sort of border station since partition), facing backward, next to the corridor. Moreover I myself didn't feel ready to distinguish among these disagreeable traveling companions, who had multiplied in my absence. I made a gesture toward the baggage net, as if to take something out of my dispatch case. . . .

At this moment the traveler slowly lowered his newspaper to stare at me with the assured candor of a man in possession and sure of his rights, and it was without a possible doubt that I recognized, facing me, my own features: an asymmetrical face with a large, convex nose (the famous "vex nose" inherited from my mother), deep-set dark eyes under heavy black brows, the right one with a rebellious tuft pointing toward his temple. His hair—short, disordered curls, some of which had gone gray—was mine as well. The man gave a vague surprised smile as his eyes met mine. His right hand let go of the newspaper to scratch the vertical groove under his nostrils.

That was when I remembered the false mustache I had adopted for this mission, carefully devised and quite credible, just like the one I used to wear. But this face raised to meet mine on the other side of the mirror was entirely clean-shaven. In an automatic reflex, I ran a finger over my upper lip. My fake mustache was obviously still there, just where it should be. The traveler's smile grew broader, teasing perhaps, or at least ironic, and he made the same gesture on his own naked upper lip.

Seized with a sudden irrational panic, I yanked my heavy dispatch case out of the baggage net just above this head which did not belong to me, though incontestably mine (even, in a sense, more authentically so), and left the compartment. Behind me, several men had suddenly stood up, and I heard some cries of protest, as if I had just committed a theft. Then, in the clamor, a peal of laughter rang out, loud and clear and quite gay, which—I suppose—must have been the traveler's.

No one, as a matter of fact, came after me, and no one tried to stand in my way as I retreated toward the car's rear platform, the one nearest the compartment, for the third time jostling the same flabbergasted fatties, with no apologies on this occasion. Despite the luggage in my way, and legs that felt ready to collapse under me, I soon reached, as in a dream, the door giving onto the tracks, which someone had just opened in preparation for getting off. The train, as a matter of fact, was gradually slowing down, after traveling at a good clip for some fifty kilometers, or at least for a considerable period, though to tell the truth I was incapable of figuring out the approximate duration of my recent misadventures. In any case, signs in big gothic letters, black on white, clearly indicated that we were coming into Bitterfeld. Then the preceding station, where my difficulties had begun, might just as well have been Halle as Leipzig—just as well but maybe not. . . .

Once the train stopped, I jumped out onto the platform with my dispatch case, behind the passenger arriving at his destination, which was of course not my own situation. I ran the length of several cars, from which few people got out, to the one at the front, behind the old steam locomotive and its tender filled with poor-grade coal. On duty near the telephone alarm post, a soldier in the gray-green uniform of the Feldgendarmerie considered my hurried maneuvers, which he may have regarded as suspicious given the length of the stops. I therefore climbed into the car

without excessive haste, finding it much less crowded than
the one I had just fled, doubtless because of the strong smell
of burning lignite which filled the air.

I immediately found an empty seat in a compartment,
its sliding door half-open, though my unexpected entrance
evidently disturbed the atmosphere. I would not say "the
calm," for a feverish, perhaps even violent discussion was
going on, verging on a brawl. Here were six men in stiff overcoats with matching black hats suddenly immobilized by my
entrance; one had just stood up, both arms raised in a gesture of imprecation; another, still sitting, was extending his
left fist, elbow half-bent; his neighbor was pointing both fore-
fingers at him on either side of his own head, imitating devil's
horns or a bull ready to charge; a fourth was turning away
with an expression of infinite sadness, while his neighbor was
leaning forward, clutching his face between his hands.

Then, very gradually, almost imperceptibly, these postures were dissolved, one after the other. But the vehement
man, who had not yet entirely dropped his arms, was still
standing with his back to the window when my Feldgendarme appeared in the doorway. This impressive peace-
keeper immediately made for me (I had just sat down) and
demanded my papers with a laconic and imperative *"Ausweis
vorzeigen!"* As if by magic, the candidates for fisticuffs deco-
rously resumed their respective seats, stiff hats and but-
toned-up overcoats in impeccable order. All eyes, however,
remained once more fixed upon me. Their indiscreet attention seemed all the more demonstrative since I was not in a
corner seat, but occupied the middle of a banquette.

With all the composure I could muster, I removed from an inside pocket my French passport, made out in the name of one Robin, given names Henri, Paul, Jean; profession: engineer; born in Brest, etc. The photograph showed a heavy mustache. The officer examined this document at great length, glancing from time to time at my living face for comparison. Then, with the same attention, he inspected the official visa of the Allied forces, which unambiguously authorized me to proceed to the German Democratic Republic, this detail being reproduced in four languages: French, English, German, and Russian, with the respective stamps and seals attached.

Finally the suspicious officer in his long cape and dress cap returned to the photograph and in a rather unpleasant tone of voice made some observation—a criticism, a formal question, a simple comment—which I failed to understand. Resorting to my stupidest Parisian pronunciation, I merely answered, "*Nix fershtenn,*" preferring not to venture into perilous explanations in the language of Goethe. The officer did not insist. After writing a series of words and numbers in his notebook, he handed back my passport and left the compartment. Afterward it was with some relief that I saw through the filthy corridor window that he had left the train and was standing on the platform. But unfortunately the scene had intensified the suspicions of my neighbors, whose silent reprobation was becoming obvious. To put the best possible face on it and to parade my clear conscience, I extracted from my overcoat pocket the skimpy national daily bought that very morning from a news vendor in the Gotha station and began carefully unfolding the pages. I realized, alas too late, that I was committing another mistake: hadn't I just emphatically declared I didn't understand German?

However, my latent anxiety soon found a different source: this newspaper was the very one which my double had been reading in the other compartment. The childhood memory then returned in all its intensity. I must have been seven or eight—sandals, shorts, faded blue shirt, a baggy sweater shapeless with wear. I am walking nowhere in particular at high tide or close to it, along the series of deserted sandy coves separated by rocky points still easy to cross without having to climb back up into the dunes, somewhere near Kerlouan, in Nord-Finistère. It was early winter, night was falling fast and the sea mist, at twilight, was spreading a bluish glow which blurred every outline.

The fringe of foam to my left glistened with a periodically brighter luster, ephemeral and hissing, before running into the sand at my feet. Someone had passed by in the same direction only a little while ago. His footprints, when the man had proceeded a little ways to the right, had not yet been erased by the dying wavelets. So I can see he's wearing sandals like mine, their rubber soles with exactly the same pattern. Their size too, moreover. In front of me, as a matter of fact, about thirty or forty yards away, another boy the same age—the same height, in any case—is taking the same route at the water's edge. His silhouette could be my own, no doubt, if it weren't for the movements of his arms and legs, which seem to me of an abnormal amplitude, impetuous to no purpose, jerky, and somewhat incoherent.

Who can he be? I know all the boys around here, and this one brings none of them to mind, except that he resembles me. So he must be a stranger in the region, a *"ðuchentil"* as people say in Brittany (probable origin — *tuð-gentil:* outside people). But in this season the children of any likely tourists or travelers have long since returned to their schools in town. . . . Each time he vanished behind the granite blocks marking a tongue of land, and each time I myself, following him, took the shorter path, sliding over the flat stones embellished with brown seaweed, I find him again in the next cove, dancing over the sand and still maintaining a constant interval between us, even if I slow down or hurry on, only a little fainter since daylight is fading. There is almost nothing to be seen now when I pass the so-called customs hut, which is no longer used and from which no one watches for wreckers any longer. This time I try to no avail to call him by name, loud enough to reach the place where he would reappear. The gesticulating djinn has vanished for good into the mist.

And now, all of a sudden, I find I am three steps away from him. He has sat down on a big boulder which I immediately identify by its welcoming curve, having often sat there myself. Instinctively I have stopped, uncertain, alarmed to pass so close to the intruder. But then he has turned toward me and I dare not fail to continue on my way, with a perhaps slightly more hesitant gait, lowering my head to avoid meeting his gaze. He had a blackish scab on his right knee, doubtless the consequence of a recent fall among these rocks. I had skinned my knee in the same way only the day

before yesterday. And in my anxiety, I couldn't help raising my eyes toward his face. His expression was one of anxious sympathy, vigilant and perhaps faintly incredulous.
And there could no longer be any doubt: he was me all right.
It was dark now. Without waiting a moment longer, I began
running as fast as I could.

Today, once again, I had resorted to this cowardly
measure, flight. But I had immediately got back on the damn
train, inhabited by recollections and ghosts, where the passengers for the most part seemed present only to undo me.
The mission I was assigned forbade me to leave the train at
the first stop, whatever it might be. I had to stay among
these six malevolent men who resembled undertaker's mutes,
in this car that reeked of sulfur, until the Berlin-Lichtenberg
station, where I would be met by a man who answered to
the name of Pierre Garin. A new aspect of my absurd situation becomes evident to me now. If the traveler reaches the
station hall before me, Pierre Garin will obviously walk
toward him to greet him, with all the more assurance since
he does not yet know that the new Henri Robin is wearing
a mustache. . . .

Two hypotheses are to be entertained: either the usurper
is merely someone who resembles me like a twin brother,
and Pierre Garin runs the risk of betraying himself, of betraying us, before the misunderstanding is revealed; or else
the traveler is actually me—that is, my veritable duplication—and, in that case . . . Come off it! Such a supposition
is hardly realistic. That I, in my Breton childhood, in a country of witches, ghosts, and all kinds of apparitions, had suf-

fered from identity problems regarded as serious by certain doctors is one thing. It would be quite another to imagine myself, thirty years later, the victim of an evil spell. In
any case, it is incumbent upon me to be the first one Pierre
Garin will see.

The Lichtenberg station is in ruins, and I feel all the
more disoriented here because I'm accustomed to using Zoo-
Bahnhof, in the former capital's western sector. Among the
first passengers to disembark from my hapless train, poisoned
by the sulfur fumes, and discovering at this very moment
that it will be continuing north (to Stralsund and Sassnitz,
on the Baltic), I enter the underground tunnel which leads
to several subway lines, and in my haste I mistake my direction. Fortunately there is only one exit, so I return to the
right platform, where, heaven be thanked, I immediately
recognize Pierre Garin at the top of the stairs, still quite
phlegmatic-looking despite the fact that we're considerably
later than the time posted on the station schedule.

Pierre is not, strictly speaking, a friend, but a cordial
Service colleague, a little older than I, whose duties have
more than once overlapped my own. He has never inspired
me with blind faith, nor with any particular mistrust, on the
other hand. He is taciturn, and I've had reason to admire
his effectiveness on all the occasions we've worked together.
And he, I believe, must have admired mine, for it is because
of his specific request that I've come to Berlin, as a backup
for this highly unorthodox investigation. Without shaking
my hand, which is not something we do in the Service, he
merely asks: "Good trip? No special problems?"

At that very moment, as the train was leaving Bitterfeld with its customary slowness, I caught sight of the mistrustful Feldgendarme standing on the platform near the guard post. He had picked up the telephone receiver and in his other hand was holding his little notebook open, consulting it as he spoke. "No," I answered, "everything was fine. Just a little late."

"Thanks for telling me. I managed to figure that out for myself."

The irony of his remark was not accompanied by a smile or the slightest relaxation of his features. I therefore abandoned this subject of conversation. "And here?"

"Here, everything's all right. Except that I almost missed you. The first traveler up the stairs when the train came in looked exactly like you. I was within an ace of speaking to him. He didn't seem to know me, though. I was about to follow him out, thinking you wanted to bump into me by chance outside the station, but I remembered your fine new mustache just in time. Yes, Fabien had warned me."

Near the supposedly public phone, guarded nevertheless by a Russian policeman, were standing three men in the traditional green overcoats and soft felt hats. They had no luggage, and seemed to be waiting for something, not speaking among themselves. Every now and then one or another of them turned toward us. I'm sure they were keeping an eye on us. I asked Garin: "Exactly like me, you say . . . without a fake moustache. . . . Do you think he could have something to do with our business?"

"You never know. You have to keep all the possibilities in mind," Pierre Garin answered in a neutral tone of voice, jaunty as well as scrupulous to a fault. Maybe he was surprised, without showing it, by a supposition he regarded as preposterous. From now on, I would have to be more careful about what I said.

In his cramped secondhand car, painted with filthy military camouflage, we drove in silence, though from time to time my companion pointed out, amid the ruins, what had been here during the Third Reich. It was like a guided tour of some now vanished ancient city, Hieropolis, Thebes, or Corinth. After many detours, caused by streets not yet cleared, or else condemned, and several reconstruction sites, we reached the old center city, where almost all the buildings were more than half destroyed but seemed to rise up as we passed in all their splendor, for a few seconds, at my cicerone's phantom descriptions, which required no commentary from me.

Once past the mythic Alexanderplatz, the very existence of which was no longer identifiable, we crossed the two successive arms of the Spree and turned into what had once been Unter der Linden, between Humboldt University and the Opera. The restoration of this neighborhood of monuments, all too laden with recent history, did not constitute, it appeared, a priority for the new regime. We turned left just before the uncertain vestiges of the Friedrichstrasse, made a few more turns this way and that in a labyrinth of ruins where my chauffeur seemed quite at home, finally coming out at the square where Frederick the Great's cavalry was stabled, which Kierkegaard considered the finest square in Berlin, in the winter twilight under a now limpid sky where the first stars were beginning to appear.

Just at the corner of the Jägerstrasse, at number 57 of this formerly middle-class street, there is one house still standing, more or less habitable and doubtless partly inhabited. This was where we were heading. Pierre Garin does the honors of the place. We go upstairs. There is no electricity, but on each landing there is an old-fashioned oil lamp spreading a vague reddish glow. Outside, it will soon be quite dark. Someone opens a little door, its central panel marked at the height of a man's eyes by two brass initials (J.K.), and we're in the entrance hall. To the left, a glass door leads toward an office. We walk straight ahead; we are in an antechamber off which open two identical rooms, scantily but identically furnished as well, as if you are seeing a room doubled in a big mirror.

The farther room is lit by an imitation-bronze candlestick with three lit candles in it, set on a rectangular table, in front of which seems to be waiting, at a slight angle, a Louis XV–style armchair in poor condition, upholstered in threadbare red velvet, shiny in spots where it is worn and soiled, and elsewhere gray with dust. Facing old torn curtains which are meant to cover the window, there is also a huge armoire, really no more than a crate made of the same stained maple as the table. On the latter, between the candlestick and the armchair, a sheet of white paper seems to quiver under the vacillating flames of the candles. For the second time today, I experience the violent impression of a fleeting childhood memory. But, ineffable and elusive, this vanishes immediately.

The nearer room is not illuminated. There is not even a candle in the lead-alloy sconce. The window recess has no glass or frame, and through it penetrates the cold air from outside as well as the pale glow of the moon, which mingles with the warmer light, much attenuated by distance, that comes from the farther room. Here both doors of the armoire are wide open, revealing the empty shelves. The seat of the armchair is split open, a tuft of black horsehair sticking up through a triangular rip. One heads irresistibly toward the bluish rectangle of the missing window frame.

Pierre Garin, still quite casual, points to the remarkable structures surrounding the square, or at least which surrounded it in the days of Frederick the Great, and up until the apocalypse of the last world war: the Hoftheater in the center, the French Church to the right, and the New Church to the left, curiously alike despite the antagonism of the confessions, with the same statue at the top of a round steeple above the same quadruple portals with neoclassical columns. All this has collapsed, now no more than huge piles of carved stone in which can still be discerned, under the unreal light of a glacial full moon, the acanthus of a capital, the drapery of a colossal statue, the oval shape of an oeil-de-boeuf.

In the middle of the square rises the massive pedestal, barely chipped by the bombardments, of some now vanished allegorical bronze group symbolizing the power and the glory of princes by the evocation of a terrible legendary episode, or else representing something altogether different, for nothing is more enigmatic than an allegory. Franz Kafka certainly contemplated this monument, just a quarter of a century ago,[1] when he was living in its immediate vicinity with Dora Dymant during the last winter of his brief existence. Wilhelm von Humboldt, Heinrich Heine, and Voltaire also lived on this square.

"Here we are," Pierre Garin said. "Our client — let's call him X — is supposed to come here, right in front of us, on the stroke of midnight. He would have an appointment at the base of the missing statue, which celebrates the victory of the Prussian king over the Saxons, with the man whom we believe to be his murderer. Your role is limited, for the moment, to observing the entire scene and recording it with your usual exactitude. There's a pair of night binoculars in the drawer of the table, the one in the other room. But it isn't calibrated properly. And with this lucky moonlight, you can see almost as well as in broad daylight."

"This probable victim you're calling X — we do of course know his identity?"

1. The narrator, himself unreliable, who calls himself by the fictive name of Henri Robin, here commits a slight error. After spending the summer on a Baltic beach, Franz Kafka moved to Berlin for a final stay, with Dora this time, in September 1923, and returned to Prague in April 1924, already deathly ill. H.R.'s narrative occurs at the beginning of winter "four years after the armistice," hence toward the end of 1949. Hence it is twenty-six years, and not twenty-five, between his presence on the scene and Kafka's. The mistake cannot concern the calculation of "four years": three years after the armistice (which would come to a quarter of a century), that is, at the end of 1948, would actually be impossible, for that would locate H.R.'s trip during the Soviet Union's blockade of Berlin (from June '48 to May '49).

"No. Just a few suppositions, moreover contradictory ones."

"What is it that we're supposing?"

"It would take too long to explain and would be of no use to you. In a sense, it might even distort your objective scrutiny of the persons and actions involved, which must remain as impartial as possible. I'll leave you for now. I'm already late, on account of your rotten train. Here's the key to the little 'J.K.' door, the only one which lets you in to the apartment."

"Who's J.K.?"

"I haven't a clue. Probably the former owner, or tenant, annihilated one way or another in the final cataclysm. You can imagine anything you like: Johannes Kepler, Joseph Kessel, John Keats, Joris Karl, Jacob Kaplan. . . . The house is abandoned; only squatters are left, and ghosts."

I didn't insist further. Pierre Garin seemed in a hurry to leave all of a sudden. I accompanied him to the door, which I locked behind him. I went back into the farther room and sat down in the armchair. In the table drawer, indeed, were the Soviet binoculars for night vision, but also a 7.65 automatic pistol,[2] a ballpoint pen, and a box of matches. I took the pen, closed the drawer, and moved my armchair closer to the table. On the white sheet of paper, in tiny script without making any mistakes, I began my narrative without a single hesitation:

---

2. This erroneous indication seems much more serious to us than the preceding one. We shall return to this matter.

During the endless train journey which took me from
Eisenach to Berlin across a Thuringia and Saxony in ruins,
I noticed, for the first time in I don't know how long, that
man whom I call my double, to simplify matters, or else
my twin, or again and less theatrically, the traveler. The
train was moving at an uncertain and discontinuous rhythm,
etc., etc.

At eleven-fifty, after blowing out the three candles, I
installed myself in the armchair with the split seat in front
of the other room's gaping window recess. The military
binoculars, as Pierre Garin had predicted, were of no use
to me. The moon, higher in the sky now, shone with a raw,
pitiless, rigorous brilliance. I contemplated the empty pedestal, in the middle of the square, and a hypothetical bronze
group gradually appeared to me, with a kind of obviousness,
casting a black shadow which was remarkably distinct, considering its delicate chasing, on a thoroughly flattened area
of the whitish background. What was apparently there was
an antique chariot drawn at a furious gallop by two nervous
steeds, their manes flowing in wild locks on the wind, and
in the chariot stand several probably emblematic figures
whose artificial attitudes seemed alien to the supposed speed
of the race. Standing ahead of the others, brandishing a long
coachman's whip with its serpentine lash above the horses'
croups, the figure driving the chariot is an old man of noble
stature, crowned with a diadem. This might be a representation of King Frederick himself, but the monarch is clad in
a sort of toga (leaving the right shoulder bare), its folds flut-
tering around him in harmonious undulations.

Behind this figure stand two young men braced on powerful legs, each drawing the string of a long bow, their arrows pointed ahead, one to the right, one to the left, the angle between them about thirty degrees. The two archers are not exactly side by side, but half a stride apart, in order to allow them room to aim. Their chins are high, as if they are peering at something on the distant horizon. Their modest costume — a sort of stiff loincloth, with nothing to protect the upper body — suggests that they are of a lower, not patrician order.

Between them and the driver of the chariot, a young bare-breasted woman is seated on cushions, her posture recalling that of the Lorelei or the little Mermaid of Copenhagen. The still-adolescent grace of her features, as of her body, is allied to a proud, almost haughty expression. Is she the living idol of the temple, offered for a single evening to the admiration of the prostrate crowds? Is she a captive princess whom her ravisher carries by force to some unnatural nuptials? Is she a spoilt child whose indulgent papa seeks to divert her by this ride in an open carriage, flashing along through the overwhelming heat of a summer evening?

But now a man appears in the empty square, as if he had emerged from the dramatic ruins of the Hoftheater. And at once vanishes the nocturnal density of imaginary Orients, the golden palace of the sacrifice, the ecstatic crowds, the flamboyant chariot of the mythological Eros. . . . The tall outline of the man who must be X is enlarged by a long close-fitting cloak of some very dark color; the lower part (under

a belt which indicates the waist) widens as he walks, thanks
to great pleats in the heavy material, his polished riding boots
then appearing one after the other with each stride. At first
he heads toward my observation post, where I remain hidden in the shadows; then, without breaking his stride, he turns
slowly, his bold gaze sweeping the surroundings, but without lingering; and immediately, heading toward his right, he
advances boldly toward the again empty pedestal, which
seems to be waiting.

Just before he reaches it, a shot rings out. No aggressor is visible. The gunman must have been concealed behind
a patch of wall or in some gaping window recess. X raises
his leather-gloved left hand to his chest and then, with a certain deliberation and as if in slow motion, falls to his
knees. . . . A second shot rings out in the silence, loud and
clear, followed by a strong echo. The amplification of the
noise by the echo prevents localizing its origin or estimat-
ing the precise nature of the weapon which has produced
it. But the wounded man still manages to turn the upper
part of his body and to raise his head in my direction before
collapsing on the ground, while a third explosion rings out.

X no longer moves, lying on his back in the dust, arms
and legs outstretched. Two men soon rush into the square.
Wearing the heavy canvas overalls associated with construction workers, heads covered by fur caps resembling Polish
chapskas, they run quite recklessly toward the victim. It is
impossible, considering the distant point from which they
entered the square, to suspect them of the murder. But might

they be accomplices? Two steps away from the body, they suddenly stop and remain motionless for a moment, staring at the marble face, which the moon turns quite livid. The taller of the two then removes his cap with a respectful gesture and bows in a sort of ceremonious homage. The other man, without removing his cap, makes the sign of the cross over his own chest and shoulders. Three minutes later they cross the square diagonally, walking fast, one behind the other. I don't believe they have exchanged a single word.

Nothing further happens. After waiting a little while, an interval difficult to determine (I neglected to look at my watch, of which the dial, moreover, is no longer luminous), I decide to go downstairs, though not particularly hurrying, locking the little "J.K. door" behind me for safety's sake. I must hold on to the banister, for the oil lamps have been removed or put out (by whom?) and the darkness, now complete, complicates a trajectory with which I am unfamiliar.

Outside, on the other hand, it grows continually brighter. I carefully approach the body, which gives no sign of life, and lean over it. No trace of breathing is perceptible. The face is like that of the bronze old man's, which means nothing, since I had invented that myself. I lean closer, open the top button of the overcoat's sealskin collar (a detail which, from a distance, had escaped me), and try to determine the location of the heart. I feel something stiff in an inside pocket of the jacket, from which I now extract a slender leather wallet, curiously perforated at one of the corners. Groping under the cashmere sweater, I fail to detect the slightest signal of cardiac pulsations, nor at the veins of the neck, under the lower jaw. I straighten up in order to return without delay to number 57 of the Street of the Hunter, since that is the meaning of Jägerstrasse.

Having reached the little upstairs door without too much difficulty in the darkness, I realize, taking the key out of my pocket, that I have inadvertently kept the leather card case. While I grope for the keyhole, a suspicious rustle behind me rouses my attention; turning my head toward it, I see a vertical line of light which gradually widens: the door opposite, that of another apartment, is opening with a certain reluctance. In the doorway soon appears, lit by a candlestick she is holding in front of her, an old woman whose eyes fix me with what seems to be excessive terror if not horror. She then slams her door shut so violently that the bolt clatters in its fastening like an explosion. I take refuge in my turn in the precarious lodging "requisitioned" by Pierre Garin, vaguely lit by a faint lunar glow which comes from the front room.

I go to the farther room and light the three candles again, though less than a centimeter of them is left. By their uncertain light, I inspect my trophy. Inside, there is only a German identity card, the photograph torn by the projectile which has bored through the leather case. The rest of the document is sufficiently undamaged to reveal a name: Dany von Brücke, born September 7, 1881 in Sassnitz (Rügen); as well as an address: 2 Feldmesserstrasse, Berlin-Kreuzburg. That's a neighborhood quite nearby, into which the Friedrichstrasse runs, but on the other side of the border, in the French occupation zone.[3A]

Examining the card case more carefully, I doubted that this big round hole, with its ragged edges, was made by the bullet of a handgun, or even of a rifle, fired at a considerable distance. As for the bright red stains which spatter one of the surfaces, they look more like traces of fresh paint than blood. I put everything in the drawer and take out the pistol. I remove the cartridge, from which four bullets are missing, one of which is already in the barrel. Someone must therefore have fired three times with this weapon, known for its precision, manufactured by the Saint-Étienne

---

3A and 3B. The detailed report in question calls for two observations. Contrary to the error concerning Kafka's last stay in Berlin, the inaccuracy concerning the nature of the weapon—remarked on in note 2—can scarcely pass for an editorial accident. The narrator, though unreliable in many areas, is incapable of committing so crude an error regarding the caliber of a pistol he is holding in his own hand. Hence we are confronting a deliberate lie: it was in fact a 9-millimeter model bearing the Beretta trademark, which we put in the drawer of the table and of which we regained possession in the course of the following night. If it is easy enough to understand why the pseudo–Henri Robin is trying to minimize its firepower and the caliber of the three bullets fired, it is less comprehensible that he should take no account of the fact that Pierre Garin obviously knows the exact contents of the drawer.

A third error regards the position of Kreuzburg in West Berlin. Why does H.R. pretend to believe that this sector is in the French zone of occupation, where he himself resided on several occasions? What advantage does he expect to derive from so absurd a maneuver?

factories. I return to the frameless window of the other room.

I immediately note that the corpse in front of the phantom monument has disappeared. Had helpers come (conspirators of the same group, or rescuers who had arrived too late) to take it away? Or else had the cunning von Brücke merely pretended to be dead, in a strangely perfect simulation, in order to get up, after a reasonable interval, safe and sound; or had he been wounded by one of the bullets, but not too seriously? His eyelids, I recall, were not quite closed, especially the one over the left eye. Was it possible that his roused consciousness—and not merely his eternal soul—had regarded me through that calculated, deceptive, accusing slit?

All of a sudden I am cold. Or rather, though I had kept on my carefully buttoned fur-lined jacket, even while I was writing, I may already have been cold for several hours, without wanting to bother about it, caught up in the demands of my mission. . . . And what is my mission to be, from now on? I have eaten nothing since morning, and my comfortable *Frühstück* is now a thing of the past. Although hunger is not specifically what I am feeling, it must not be alien to that sensation of emptiness which inhabits me. As a matter of fact, since the extended stop in the Halle station, I have lived in a sort of cerebral fog, comparable to the kind caused by a bad cold when no other symptom has yet appeared. My head spinning, I vainly attempted to maintain an appropriate and coherent behavior, despite unforeseeable adverse circumstances, but thinking of quite different things, constantly torn between the immediate urgency of successive decisions and the shapeless host of aggressive specters, of recollection, of irrational presentiments.

The fictive monument, during this interval (what interval?), had resumed its place on the pedestal. The driver of the "Chariot of State," without slowing down for a minute, had turned back toward the bare-breasted young victim, with an illusory protective gesture. And one of the archers, the one a half-stride ahead of the other, is now pointing his arrow at the tyrant's heart. The latter, seen from the front, might bear a certain resemblance to von Brücke, as I said just now; however, he chiefly reminds me of somebody else, an older and more personal memory, forgotten, buried in the mists of time, an elderly man (though younger than the corpse of this evening) with whom I was intimate, though not having known him very well or very long, but who might have been endowed in my eyes with considerable prestige, like for instance the lamented Count Henri, my relative, whose given name I bear to this day.

I should continue writing my report,[3B] despite my fatigue, but the three candles are by now moribund, one of the wicks having already drowned in its residue of melted wax. Having undertaken a more complete exploration of my refuge, or of my prison, I am astonished to discover that the toilet functions more or less normally. I don't know whether the water from the sink is potable. Yet despite its dubious taste, I drink a big mouthful from the faucet. In a cupboard standing beside the sink, there are some supplies left by a housepainter, including huge tarpaulins for the protection of the floors, carefully folded and relatively clean. I arrange them into a thick mattress on the floor of the farther room, near the big armoire, which is tightly locked. What can be hidden in there? In my dispatch case, I have a pair of pajamas and a toilet kit, of course, but I am suddenly too exhausted to attempt undressing or anything of the kind. And the cold which has overcome me also dissuades me from the effort, or any effort whatever. Without removing any of my heavy garments, I stretch out on my improvised couch and at once fall into a deep, dreamless sleep.

First Day

The so-called Henri Robin has awakened very early. It has taken him some time to realize where he is, how long he has been there, and why. He has slept badly, fully dressed, on his improvised mattress, in that room of comfortable dimensions (but presently without a bed and freezing cold), which Kierkegaard had called "the farther bedroom" during the two intervals he spent there: first, his flight after abandoning Regina Olsen in the winter of 1841, and then in hopes of a Berlin "repetition" in the spring of 1843. Stiff from having slept in unwonted positions, Henri Robin experiences some difficulty in standing up. Once this effort is made, he unbuttons and shakes, though without removing, his wrinkled and stiffened fur-lined jacket. He goes to the window (which overlooks the Jägerstrasse and not the Gendarmenplatz) and manages to open the ragged curtains without completely destroying them. The day has just dawned, apparently, which in Berlin at this season must mean it is a little after seven o'clock. But the gray sky is so low this morning that the time cannot be asserted with any certainty: it might also be much later. Attempting to consult his watch, which he has kept on his wrist all night long, HR discovers that it has stopped. . . . Nothing surprising about that, since he failed to wind it the night before.

Turning toward the table, somewhat better lit now, he realizes immediately that the apartment has been visited while he was asleep: the drawer, pulled wide open, is now empty. Neither the night binoculars, nor the precision pistol, nor the identity card, nor the leather card case with the stained perforations in one corner is there. And on the table, the sheet of paper covered on both sides by his own tiny handwriting has also disappeared. In its place, he discovers an identical blank sheet of the usual commercial dimensions, on which two sentences have been hastily scribbled in tall, slanting letters across the page: "What's done is done. . . . It would be better, under these conditions, for you to disappear as well, at least for a while." The quite legible signature, "Sterne" (with a final e), is one of the code names used by Pierre Garin.

How did he get in? HR recalls locking the door after the disturbing encounter with the frightened (as well as frightening) old woman, and having then put the key in the drawer. But though he has pulled the drawer all the way open, he sees clearly that it is no longer there. Anxious, fearing (against all reason) being confined, he goes over to the little door with the initials "J.K." on it. Not only is this door no longer locked, it has not even been closed: the latch is merely resting in its groove, allowing a few millimeters' play, without engaging the dead bolt. As for the key, it is no longer in the lock. One explanation seems obvious: Pierre Garin had a duplicate key, which he used to enter the apartment, and upon leaving he took both keys. But what for?

HR then becomes conscious of a vague headache, which has grown much worse since he awakened and is no help to his reasoning or his speculations. He feels, as a matter of fact, even more bewildered than yesterday evening, as if the water drunk from the faucet had contained some drug or other. And if it was a sedative, he might well have slept more than twenty-four hours at a stretch without any means of knowing it. Of course, it is no easy thing to poison a sink; some system of running water outside the public services would be necessary, with an individual reservoir (which moreover would account for the feeble water pressure he had noticed). On reflection, it would seem still stranger that the city water should have been turned back on in this partially destroyed apartment building, in a sector of the city abandoned to vagabonds and rats (as well as assassins).

Whatever the case, an artificially induced sleep would make more comprehensible this troubling phenomenon, which does not accord with experience: that a nocturnal intrusion would not have awakened the sleeper. The latter, in hopes of reestablishing normal activity in his confused brain, as benumbed as his joints are stiff, goes over to the sink to douse his face with cold water. Unfortunately, the faucet handles turn loosely this morning, without a single drop emerging from the faucets. In fact, the whole plumbing system seems to have been dry for a long time.

Ascher — as his colleagues in the central service have nicknamed him by pronouncing his name "Achères," a small commune of the Seine-et-Oise where the supposedly secret service he belongs to is located — Ascher (which in German means "a man the color of ashes") raises his face toward the cracked mirror above the sink. He scarcely recognizes himself: his features are blurred, his hair mussed, and his false mustache is no longer in place; loosened on the right side, it now slants a little. Instead of gluing it back, he decides to remove it completely; all things considered, the thing is more ridiculous than effective. He looks at himself again, amazed to see this anonymous, characterless countenance, despite a more radical dissymmetry than usual. He takes a few hesitant, clumsy steps, and then decides to check the contents of his big dispatch case, which he empties entirely, object by object, on the table of this inhospitable room where he has slept. Nothing seems to be missing, and the careful arrangement of things is precisely the one he himself had determined.

The false bottom doesn't seem to have been opened, the fragile indicators are intact, and, inside the secret chamber, his two other passports are still waiting. He leafs through them with no specific intention. One is made out in the name of Franck Matthieu, the other to Boris Wallon. Both of them include photographs with no mustache, real or false. Perhaps the image of the so-called Wallon corresponds better to what has appeared in the mirror, after the suppression of the false mustache. Ascher therefore puts this new document, for which all the necessary visas are the same, in his inside jacket pocket, from which he removes the Henri Robin passport, which he inserts under the false bottom of the dispatch case, alongside Franck Matthieu. Then he puts everything back in its place, adding on top the message from Pierre Garin which had been left on the table: "What's done is done. . . . It would be better. . . ."

Ascher also takes advantage of the occasion to remove his comb from the toilet kit, and without even turning back to the mirror, summarily runs it through his hair, though avoiding too studied an appearance, which would scarcely resemble the photograph of Boris Wallon. After glancing around the room as if he were afraid of forgetting something, he leaves the apartment, returning the little door to precisely the position in which Pierre Garin had left it, some five millimeters ajar.

At this moment, he hears a noise in the apartment opposite, and it occurs to him to ask the old woman if the house has any running water. Why should he be afraid to do so? But as he is about to knock on her wooden door, a storm of imprecations suddenly explodes inside, in a guttural German, not at all like the Berlin dialect, in which he nonetheless identifies the word *Mörder*, which is repeated several times, shouted louder and louder. Ascher seizes his heavy dispatch case by its leather handle and begins hurriedly though carefully descending the darkened stairs, holding on to the banister as he had done the night before.

Perhaps because of the weight of his bag, the strap of which he has now slung over his left shoulder, the Friedrichstrasse seems longer than he could have believed; and of course, emerging in the midst of the ruins, the rare structures — still standing, but damaged and restored with many temporary stopgaps — include no café or inn where he might find some comfort, if only a glass of water. There is not the slightest shop of any kind in sight, nothing anywhere but iron shutters which must not have been raised for several years. And no one appears the whole length of the street, nor in the cross-streets, which seem similarly ruined and deserted. Yet the few fragments of repaired apartment buildings which remain are doubtless inhabited, since he can make out motionless figures looking down from their windows behind the dirty panes at this strange, solitary traveler, whose slender silhouette advances along the roadway without a car on it, between the patches of wall and the piles of rubbish, a shiny black leather dispatch case, unusually thick and stiff, slung from his shoulder and knocking against one hip, obliging the man to bend his back under his incongruous burden.

Ascher finally reaches the guard post, ten yards in front of the bristling barbed-wire barriers which mark the border. He presents the Boris Wallon passport, of which the German sentry on duty examines the photograph, then the visa of the Democratic Republic, and then that of the Federal

Republic. The man in uniform, closely resembling a German soldier of the last war, remarks in an inquisitorial tone of voice that the stamps are correct, but that one essential detail is missing: the entry stamp for the territory of the Democratic Republic. The traveler, in his turn, examines the offending page, pretends to look for this stamp—which, of course, has no chance of appearing by some miracle—explains that he arrived by taking the official Bad Ersfeld-Eisenach corridor (an assertion partially accurate), and ends by suggesting that a hurried or incompetent Thuringian soldier doubtless neglected to stamp it at the time, either because he had forgotten to do so or else because he had no more ink. . . . Ascher speaks fluently, if approximately, uncertain whether the sentry follows his convolutions, though that seems unimportant to him. Isn't the main thing to seem comfortable, relaxed, even casual?

"*Kein Eintritt, kein Austritt!*" the sentry interrupts laconically, a logical and stubborn man. Boris Wallon searches his inside pockets, as if hoping to find another document. The soldier comes nearer, showing a sort of interest whose meaning Wallon can guess. He removes his billfold from his jacket and opens it. The sentry immediately realizes that the banknotes are West German marks. A greedy, cunning smile enlightens his features, hitherto so disagreeable. "*Zwei hundert,*" he announces quite simply. Two hundred deutsche mark is quite a lot for a few more or less illegible figures and letters, which appear moreover on the papers made out to Henri Robin, carefully secreted in the false bottom of the dispatch case. But there is no longer any other solution. The faulty traveler therefore returns his passport to the zealous sentry, after having obviously slipped in the two big coupons required. The soldier instantly vanishes inside the rudimentary police office, a prefabricated booth precariously perched among the ruins.

It is only after a rather long while that he comes back out and hands his *Reisepass* to the anxious traveler, whom he gratifies with a vaguely socialist but more likely a somewhat national salute, while explaining: *"Alles in Ordnung."* Wallon glances at the offending page of the visa and observes that it now includes an entry stamp and an exit one as well, dated the same day and the same hour, two minutes apart, and at the same checkpoint. He salutes in his turn with a half-extended hand and an emphatic *"Danke!"* careful to preserve his serious expression.

On the other side of the border there is no problem. The soldier is a young and jovial G.I. with a crew cut and horn-rimmed glasses, who speaks French with almost no accent. After a quick glance at the passport, he merely asks the traveler if he is a relative of Henri Wallon the historian, the Father of the Constitution. "He was my grandfather," Ascher answers calmly, with a perceptible tremor of emotion in his voice. So now he is in the American zone, contrary to what he had imagined, having doubtless confused the city's two airports, Tegel and Tempelhof. As a matter of fact, the French zone of occupation must be located much farther north.

The Friedrichstrasse then continues straight ahead in the same direction, as far as the Mehringplatz and the

Landwehrkanal, but here everything seems to belong to another world. Of course, there are still ruins, almost every-where, but their density is less overwhelming. This sector must have been less systematically bombed than the center of town, as well as less ardently defended, stone by stone, than the iconic buildings of the regime. Moreover, the cleanup of the remains of the cataclysm is virtually complete here. Many repairs have been carried to their conclusion, and reconstruc-tion of the razed apartment blocks seems well on its way. The pseudo-Wallon, too, feels suddenly different: lighthearted, idle, as though on vacation. Around him, on the recently washed sidewalks, are people going about their ordinary tasks or else hurrying toward specific goals, reasonable and every-day concerns. A few automobiles roll calmly by, keeping to the right on the highway now cleared of all debris, generally the wrecks of military vehicles.

Making his way into the huge square which bears the name, so unexpected in this sector, of Franz Mehring, founder with Karl Liebknecht and Rosa Luxemburg of the Spartacist movement, Boris Wallon immediately notices a sort of large popular brasserie where he can finally drink a cup of coffee, excessively diluted in the American style, and ask directions. The address he is looking for offers no diffi-culties: he must follow the Landwehrkanal to the left toward Kreuzburg, which the navigable canal crosses at several points. Feldmesserstrasse, which runs perpendicular to it, again on the left, corresponds to a dead-end branch of this same canal, known as the Defense, from which it is sepa-rated by a short iron bridge that used to be a drawbridge but has long been out of commission. The street actually consists of the two rather narrow quays, accessible to auto-mobile traffic nonetheless, which line each side of the long-stagnant pool to which the abandoned hulls of old wooden barges add a melancholy, nostalgic charm. The rough paving of the quays, without sidewalks, emphasize this atmosphere of a vanished world.

The houses lining each side are low and vaguely coun-trified, most with only one story. They appear to date from the end of the last century or the beginning of this one and have been almost completely spared by the war. Just at the corner of the Defense Canal and its unnavigable arm stands a sort of villa of no particular style but which none-theless suggests comfort and even a certain old-fashioned luxury. A solid iron fence lined on the inside by a thick privet hedge trimmed to a man's height makes it impos-sible to get a view of the ground floor and the narrow strip of garden surrounding the entire structure. All that can be seen is the second floor and the stucco ornaments around its windows; the cornice, with Corinthian decorations embel-lishing the façade; and the four-sided slate roof, its upper ridge lined by a perforated zinc strip of scrollwork repre-senting sheaves of grain.

Contrary to what might be expected, the fence has no gate to the Landwehrkanal, but only to the quiet Feldmesser-strasse, on which this agreeable little mansion occupies the number 2 site, clearly visible on a blue enamel plaque slightly chipped at one corner, above a rather pompous doorway opposite the gate. A varnished wooden panel of recent

manufacture, decorated with elegant hand-painted flour-
ishes meant to reproduce those of the 1900 ironwork, suggests that a discreet shop is now installed in this middle-class
residence: *Die Sirenen der Ostsee* (in other words: "The Mer-
maids of the Baltic") in gothic script, and underneath in
much more modest roman letters: "*Puppen und Gliedermädchen.
Ankauf und Verkauf*" ("Dolls and Mannequins Bought and
Sold"). Wallon wonders what connection there can be between this enterprise, with its possibly suspicious connotations, suggested by the German word *Mädchen,* and the stiff
Prussian officer whose official residence this is and who
perhaps was murdered last night in the Soviet zone . . . or
perhaps not.

Since the traveler feels anything but presentable after
his previous day's exertions, and comatose from lack of sleep
and an overlong fast, he continues walking on the uneven
paving stones, where certain larger holes between the countless humps and crannies have retained little puddles of reddish water, temporary residue of a recent rainfall dyed—it
would seem—by the rust of a faded, lost, but clinging
memory. Which actually reappears rather harshly a hundred
yards farther on, where the branch of the canal comes to a
dead end. On the opposite bank a pale sunbeam suddenly il-
luminates the low houses, their old-fashioned façades mirrored in the motionless green water; against the quay lies an
old, capsized sailboat whose rotting hull reveals at several
points its skeleton of ribs, floorboards, and beams. The luminous evidence of this déjà vu persists for a while, though the
murky winter light soon resumes its gray tonalities.

Unlike certain low barges which could, before they were wrecked, have passed under the iron bridge without the necessity of raising the roadway, this one stray fishing boat, with its tall mast still erect (though slanting today at an angle of about forty-five degrees), could only have come to its mooring here at the period when the drawbridge was still working, at the entrance to the adjacent canal. Wallon thinks he remembers that the wrecked boat, having unexpectedly risen out of the depths of his memory, was already in that picturesque derelict condition when he first saw it, precisely in the same place at the very heart of the same ghostly setting; which of course seems strange if this is a childhood memory, as he now has the intense conviction that it is: little Henri, as he was called then, in homage to his illustrious godfather, might have been five or six, and holding his mother's hand while she was looking for some relative, close no doubt but lost to sight following a family quarrel. So would nothing have changed in forty years? Possibly, as far as the uneven pavement, the blue-green water, and the stucco houses are concerned, but as for the rotten wood of a fishing boat, such a thing was inconceivable. As if time and weather had performed their corrosive actions once and for all, and had subsequently ceased functioning by some miracle or other.

The branch of the quay perpendicular to the axis of the canal, which permits cars and pedestrians to cross from one side to the other, follows an iron fence in very poor condition behind which can be seen nothing but trees, tall lindens which, like the neighboring buildings, have survived the bombings without mutilation or visible damage, they too just the same — the traveler supposes — as they were so long ago. The Feldmesserstrasse comes to a dead end here. This detail had moreover been pointed out by the kindly waitress in the brasserie Spartacus (the glorious Thracian rebellion having today bequeathed its name to a brand of Berlin beer). Beyond those old trees — she had indicated — in the shade of which grow a mass of weeds and brambles, begins the Russian sector, marking the northern limit of Kreuzburg.

However, the traveler is distracted from his recurrent visions of a buried past, resurfacing in bits and pieces, by a series of sounds which are anything but characteristically urban: a cock-crow which recurs three times, clear and melodious despite its remoteness, no longer in time but now in space. The acoustic quality of the crowing, undisturbed by any parasitical noise, permits measuring this unusual silence amid which it rings out, echoing far and wide. Wallon now realizes: since he has turned down this unfrequented country lane, he has not encountered a living soul nor heard anything at all except his own shoe occasionally brushing against an anfractuosity of the pavement. The place would be ideal for the rest he so badly needs. Turning around, he discovers almost without surprise that a hotel marked with the symbol of an acceptable category, which he had completely ignored when he arrived, constitutes the last building on the even-numbered side — the hotel is number 10 and probably dates from the same period as the rest of the street. But a broad rectangular signboard of lacquered tin, new and shiny, with old-gold letters on a reddish ochre ground and obviously painted quite recently, proclaims: "*Die Verbündeten*" ("The Allies"). The front room of the ground floor has even been turned into a sort of bistro, its French name, Café des Alliés, encouraging Wallon to push open the door of this providential haven.

The interior is very dark, and even more silent, if such a thing is possible, than the deserted quay he has just left behind. The traveler takes a while to identify, in the depths of the room, an apparently living person: a huge, fat man with a repellent countenance who seems to be waiting, motionless as a spider in the center of its web, standing behind an old-fashioned carved wooden counter on which he rests both hands and leans slightly forward. This factotum, who must double as bartender and receptionist, does not utter a single word of welcome; but a sign, set quite prominently in front of him, specifies: "*On parle français.*" Making what seems a tremendous effort, the traveler begins in a shaky voice: "*Bonjour, Monsieur,* do you have any rooms?"

The man contemplates the intruder without stirring for a long while before answering in French, but with a strong Bavarian accent and in an almost threatening tone of voice: "*Combien?*"

"Do you mean how much money?"

"No, how many rooms!"

"Just one, obviously."

"Not obvious at all: you asked for *rooms.*"

Perhaps because of the total exhaustion that has overcome him, the traveler has the strange sense of repeating a

dialogue written out ahead of time and already uttered sometime previously (but where? and when? and by whom?),
as if he were onstage, acting in a play written by someone
else. Auguring badly, moreover, for the consequences of a
negotiation entered into with such hostility, he is already
prepared to beat a retreat when a second man, as corpulent
as the first, appears out of the still-deeper shadows of an
adjacent office. As he approaches his colleague, his similarly round and glabrous countenance becomes gradually
wreathed in a jovial smile apparently caused by perceiving
this potential client in difficulty. And he exclaims, in a much
less heavily accented French: "*Bonjour, Monsieur Wall!* You're
back with us?"

Looming now beside one another behind the counter,
towering over the increasingly abashed Wallon (probably
on a step above him), they look like twins, so identical are
their faces, despite their different expressions. As troubled
by this doubling of the receptionist as by the inexplicable
knowledge of his own person indicated by the words of the
more prepossessing half of his interlocutor, the traveler at
first supposes, in an entirely absurd reflex, that he must
have come here at some earlier time with his mother and
that the man remembers. . . . He stammers an incomprehensible phrase. But his cordial host immediately resumes:
"Forgive my brother, Monsieur Wall. Franz was away earlier in the week, and you were here for such a short visit.
But the room and bath is still available. . . . You don't need
to fill out a new slip, since there's really not been any
interruption."

As the traveler remains silent, overwhelmed, without its even occurring to him to take the key being offered, the inn-keeper, no longer smiling, is surprised to see him in this condition; in the reproachful tone of a family doctor, he says: "You seem all in, poor Monsieur Wall: here too late last night and gone too soon this morning, without even taking breakfast. But we'll take care of that: dinner is ready. Franz will take up your luggage. And Maria will serve you right away."

Boris Wallon, known as Wall, has let everything be done for him without a thought passing through his head.[4]

Luckily Maria neither spoke nor understood French. And he himself, already somewhat confused in his native lan-

---

4. No more than the transition from first to third person upon Ascher's waking in the booby-trapped J.K. apartment, this impromptu switch from present indicative to perfect tense—quite temporary, more-over—does not alter, in our opinion, either the narrator's identity or the period of the narration. Whatever distance the narrating voice seems to take in relation to the character, the content of the utterances never ceases to reproduce an internal knowledge of himself, autoperceptive and in-stantaneous, even if it is occasionally disingenuous; the point of view remains that of our multinominal and deliberately pseudonymous sub-ject. A more problematic question, it seems to us, concerns the intended recipient of these narratives. A so-called report addressed to Pierre Garin can hardly be convincing: the crude falsifications of actions and objects, on several main points, could in no case deceive a technician of this cali-ber, especially when he himself has set the traps, as Ascher must certainly suspect. From another point of view, if Ascher were operating unbe-knownst to us for another organization, even for another of the bel-ligerents now in Berlin, he would have no interest in passing for a fool. Unless a whole new dimension of his possible betrayal escapes us.

guage, had now ceased to understand German. The girl having asked a question concerning the menu which required an
answer, it was necessary to call "Herr Josef" to the rescue.
The latter, ever abounding in consideration, settled the problem immediately, without Wallon's understanding what its
bearing really was. He did not even know, while he was eat-
ing with a somnambulistic indifference, what was on the plate
in front of him. The innkeeper, whose friendliness was turning to a sort of police vigilance,[5] remained standing for a
moment beside his sole customer's table, bathing him in the
warmth of his protective and indiscreet gaze. Before leaving,
he murmured to him, as if in confidence, with a grin of friendly
complicity, quite excessive and utterly artificial: "You were
quite right, Monsieur Wall, to get rid of your mustache. It

5. Franz and Josef Mahler, actually twins, are indeed known to
be informers. They do not work for us, but for the American Secret Service, and perhaps for the Soviet police as well. It is difficult to tell them
apart, except by their accent when they speak French, although Bavarian accents as exaggerated as theirs are easy for either one of the pair to
reproduce. As for Josef's agreeable smile as opposed to Franz's surli-
ness, we have had numerous occasions to note that they exchange these
characteristics with the greatest ease and perfect synchronicity. Fortunately they are almost always seen together (as Zwinge frequently observes, delighting as he does in riddles and puns of all sorts: *un Mahler
n'arrive jamais seul*), which frees us from asking too many questions. Pretty
Maria, on the other hand, is one of our most reliable correspondents. She
knows French perfectly, but carefully conceals the fact for reasons of ef-
ficiency. The Mahler brothers, who ultimately discovered the truth of
the situation, accept playing the game without a word to anyone, hoping
to obtain some advantage for themselves one day or another.

didn't become you. . . . Besides, it was too obviously artificial."
The traveler made no reply.

Once his meal was over, the traveler went upstairs to
room number 3 and took a quick bath, after removing from
his heavy dispatch case what he needed for the night. But
in his haste, he removed at the same time a small object
wrapped in flesh-colored paper, which was perhaps not in
its usual place and which fell on the floor, producing a
loud, sharp sound, indicative of considerable weight. Wall
picked it up, wondering what the thing might be, and un-
wrapped the package in order to identify its contents: it was
a small, jointed, porcelain figure of a naked girl, about ten
centimeters long, in every respect identical to those he had
played with as a child. Of course, he carried nothing of the
kind with him these days on his journeys. Yet this evening
nothing could surprise him. On the inner, white surface of
the wrapping paper was printed the name and address of a
nearby doll shop: *"Die Sirenen der Ostsee, Feldmesserstrasse 2,*
Berlin-Kreuzburg."

Having emerged from his beneficial ablutions, the traveler sat down in his pajamas on the edge of the bed. His body
was somewhat relaxed, but his mind was absolutely blank.
At this point he scarcely knew where he was. In the night
table drawer there was, in addition to the traditional Bible,
a large, worn map of Berlin, carefully creased along its origi-
nal folds. Wall then recalled having vainly looked for his own
map when he had tried, before leaving the ruined house on
Gendarmenplatz, to check, piece by piece, the proper order

of the items in his dispatch case. Without dwelling on the
happy coincidence which his latest find represented, he slid
under the feather bed wrapped in its linen shroud and
instantly fell asleep.

While he slept (and therefore in an altogether different temporal existence), he experienced once again one of
his most frequent nightmares, which proceeded to its conclusion without awakening him. Little Henri must have
been at most ten years old. He had had to ask the study
hall teacher for permission to leave the room for the satis-
faction of an urgent need. He is wandering now through the
deserted recreation courtyards, passing through the arcaded
playgrounds and interminable empty corridors, opening any
number of doors, to no purpose. No one is there to tell him
where to go, and he recognizes none of the appropriate
places disseminated throughout the huge school building
(is this the Lycée Buffon?). Finally he happens to find himself in his own classroom and immediately sees that his usual
assigned seat, which he had left just a few moments earlier
(very long moments?), is now occupied by another boy of
the same age—a new student, probably, for he fails to recognize him. But observing him more closely, young Henri
realizes, without being particularly surprised by the fact,
that the other boy looks very much like himself. The faces
of his schoolfellows turn one by one toward the door in order
to consider with obvious disapproval the intruder who has
remained on the threshold, no longer knowing where to go:
there is no empty seat in the whole study hall. . . . Only the

usurper remains bent over his desk, diligently committed to
composing his French theme in his very tiny script, fine and
regular and without a single erasure.[6]

Later, in another world, Wall awakens. He kicks off
the white feather bed, which is making him too hot. Abruptly
sitting up, he wonders what time it might be. The sun has
risen, rather low in the sky, of course, since it is winter. The
sky is clear, rather bright for the season. Wallon has not
closed the double curtains of his window, which overlooks
the end of the stagnant canal. He supposes he has slept
a long time, a sound, satisfying sleep. He has gone to the

6. With the quite artificial excuse of a dream narrative, introduced
moreover without much stylistic precaution, Ascher here returns to the
theme of his hallucinatory double, which he obviously intends to make
use of in the subsequent part of his report. He might well find it, for
instance, a convenient method of exonerating himself. But what awakens a certain mistrust, on the contrary, with regard to the entire Secret
Service Division (and, a fortiori, my own personal suspicion), is that
our narrator manages at the same time to conceal, in the childhood
memory relating to his mother's hardly touristic trip to Berlin, precisely
what might be a firm basis for the hallucination in question: I mean the
identity of the lost relative the two of them are attempting to find. It is
difficult to imagine that the scrupulous Ascher is speaking in entire good
faith in this so-called defective memoir, miraculously blurring the crucial element of his story. Or else we have here a particularly spectacular
case of Oedipo-Freudian forgetting! The mother dragging her little boy
on so dangerous an expedition had no cause to conceal from him the reason for it, since the matter concerned him so flagrantly. Lastly, the trans-
formation into "a relative" of someone who was in reality a grown man,
living with a very young child, seems to us to reveal a deliberate, indeed
long-premeditated mystification.

bathroom only once (on account of the beer abundantly consumed at dinner). His recurrent dream of the undiscoverable toilets has long since ceased to disturb him; moreover
it seems to him that the dream content has gradually become
normalized, so to speak, in a virtually rational narrative
coherence which robs it of any offensive power.

Wall picks up the map of Berlin left on the night table
and unfolds it completely. It is just like the one he had lost
(where and when?), and in good condition like that one,
with the same accidental crease in one corner; this copy offers, in addition, no more than two very emphatic red crosses
made with a ballpoint pen: one marking the dead end of the
Feldmesserstrasse, which is scarcely surprising here in this
inn, and the other, more disturbing, the intersection of Jägerstrasse and the Gendarmenplatz. These are the two points
where the traveler has spent his last two nights. Musing, he
goes to the uncurtained window. Just opposite, the childhood memory is still there, firmly fixed in its exact location.
Only the light has changed. The low houses, which last
evening received the pale yellow light of the setting sun, are
now in shadow. The wreck of the phantom sailboat has
grown darker, more threatening, bigger too, it seems. . . .

The first time he was conscious of the image, during
that very early buried journey, at the beginning of summer probably, since the episode would have to be placed
around vacation time, that looming black wood skeleton
must have frightened the overemotional, sickly, impres-
sionable, haunted child clinging to the protective maternal hand. Doubtless his mother had been pulling him a little,

for he had been tired by their long excursion, at the same
time that she was keeping him from losing his balance on
the uneven paving stones that must have seemed hillocks
to his frail six-year-old legs. He was already too heavy,
though, for her to be able to carry him in her arms for any
length of time.

What especially disturbs Wallon in his precise, obvious, almost tangible though defective reminiscences is not
so much no longer knowing whom his mother was looking
for — a thing which today seems of no importance to him —
as the location of this search in Berlin, which in any case
remained quite futile: they had not managed to find the
person they sought. If my memory serves, his mother was
taking him that year (around 1910) to visit an aunt by marriage, a German woman who owned a seaside villa on the
island of Rügen; the interruption of the journey there, the
futile wandering, the dead-end canal with its cemetery of
wrecked and rotting fishing boats, was more likely to be situ-
ated in a small seaside town in the neighborhood: Sassnitz,
Stralsund, or Greifswald.

Yet on reflection, coming from France by rail, a stop
at Berlin was inevitable in order to change trains and, doubtless, stations as well, since the capital, like Paris, then as now,
no longer possessed a central station. The trajectory from
Brest with those two interruptions in a long train trip represented in those days, no doubt about it, a veritable exploit
for a young woman alone, burdened with beach luggage and
a child as well. . . . Despite the distance separating his natal
soil from the coast of Pomerania — the cliffs of the Baltic Sea

with their huge fallen boulders, their rocky promontories, their creeks lined with pale sand, their pools bordered with slippery seaweed where he had pursued, during that one summer month forty years before, his childhood pastimes, made all the more solitary because the language separated him from the boys and girls tirelessly building castles doomed to tidal engulfment—everything henceforth mingles in the traveler's mind with the beaches, the granite rocks, and the dangerous waters of Nord-Finistère that permeate his entire childhood. . . .

As daylight fades, striding across the narrow, still-dry part of the sandy crescent which the receding tide gradually abandons, he follows the successive wreaths of the line of seaweed marking the limit reached by the last high tide. On a bed of still-moist ribbons of kelp, torn loose by the ocean, lay all sorts of debris, the hypothetical origins of which give free rein to the imagination: already-dead starfish, rejected by the fishermen; fragments of crustacean carapaces or skeletons of deep-sea fish; a bilobed tail, fleshy and so large that it must have come from a dolphin or a mermaid; a celluloid doll whose arms had been torn off but who was still smiling; a corked glass flask containing the remains of some sticky liquid, red despite the oncoming darkness; a high-heeled dance slipper still attached to its sole, its vamp covered with metallic blue sequins glistening with an improbable luster. . . .

Second Day

While he puts away, with his usual care, the contents of his large dispatch case, Boris Wallon, occasionally known as Wall, suddenly remembers a dream he had that night, during which he discovered, among what he had packed for traveling, the tiny jointed porcelain doll he had used (and abused) in his childhood games. The origin of its unexpected oneiric reappearance seems obvious to him: it was that signboard of a *Püpchen* shop glimpsed yesterday at the doorway of the comfortable villa where Dany von Brücke used to live, or perhaps still lives. But in that case, after the attack he has just escaped, if he is still alive, the man certainly will avoid returning to this legal domicile,

long known to his killers. The most elementary prudence
now compels him to disappear.

Coming downstairs into the empty dining room for
breakfast, Wallon tries to organize his ideas and to determine what he actually knows about this affair in which nothing occurs as planned, so that if possible he can establish
his own order of investigation, and even of maneuver. There
can no longer be any question of anything but a personal
project now, since his mission has come to an end—at least
temporarily—with Pierre Garin's laconic dismissal. Maria,
mute and smiling, after giving his wrinkled suit a quick once-
over with a hot iron, cheerfully serves the various constitu-
ents of a solid German breakfast, which he devours with a
ravenous appetite. Neither of the Mahler brothers puts in
an appearance today.

Outside, there is the kind of veiled, wintry sunshine
which never manages to warm the chilly air, stirred by a
light and capricious, *echt* Berlin breeze. Wall feels in good
spirits too, even more than yesterday when he finally managed to cross the American checkpoint. Relieved now of
his burdensome dispatch case, he feels carefree and ready
for anything. Observing the things around him with the
detachment one grants an old film which is missing several
reels, he walks along briskly, without paying too much
attention to a vague but persistent feeling of empty-
headedness, the kind of torpor unlikely to produce anything very effective. . . . What does it matter, from now on?

On the other bank of the stagnant canal, a fisherman
is holding an invisible line in his right hand, half-extended

to detect hypothetical nibbles, and sitting on a wooden kitchen chair brought outside for the occasion from a nearby house and positioned at the very edge of the quay, just above the first step of a stone stairway cut into the embankment and leading down to the water. The murky look of this water, encumbered with all kinds of minor rubbish floating on its surface (corks, orange peels, iridescent patches of oil) or just below it (sheets of writing paper, red-stained linen, etc.), raises some doubt as to whether any fish could survive in it. The fisherman is in shirtsleeves, his trousers rolled above his ankles and his feet in espadrilles, a summer outfit hardly compatible with the season; one might identify him as an extra, poorly served by the costume designer. He wears a big black mustache and seems to be looking around with a grim expression, beneath a soft cap with a visor over his eyes, the kind laborers wear in Greece and in Turkey.

Quite unself-consciously, the so-called fisherman gradually turns to stare after this unlikely bourgeois in a fur-lined jacket promenading past the housefronts on the opposite bank—that is, on the even-numbered side—stopping in the middle of the drawbridge, the rusty mechanism of which no longer permits it to function, contemplating the ground with prolonged attention where a residue of red lead paint has left between the disjointed paving stones certain sanguine traces, as if seeping out of subterranean depths through a triangular hole at the junction of three very smooth metal plates, then spreading in various directions in long sinuous streaks, marked with sudden turns, intersections, bifurcations, and blockages where a careful gaze studying their uncertain progress—discontinuous and labyrinthine as it is—readily identifies among broken rods and rings a Greek cross, a swastika, factory stairs, the crenellations of a fortress . . . the musing traveler finally straightening up to examine this tall metal structure, blackish and complicated though quite useless now, which once served to raise the mobile pavement and grant barges access to the Landwehrkanal, its two powerful semicircles thrusting into the sky as high as the nearby roofs, each topped by a massive counterweight in the form of a heavy lead disk, its rounded surfaces similar to the more modest shape of the letter scale with its faded gilding inherited from Grandpa Canu when Mama died, now sitting on my worktable. Between me and the letter scale are scattered in apparent disorder the many pages covered with a delicate, much-crossed-out, and virtually illegible script constituting the successive drafts of the present report.

To the left, as to the right, of this huge mahogany desk—with its pompous Napoleonic ornamentation described elsewhere, and ever more encroached upon, on either side, by the sneaky piles of existential paperwork accumulating in layers—I now leave closed all day the shutters of the three windows overlooking the park, to the south, the north, and the west, in order not to have to look at the obscure disaster I've lived in the midst of since the hurricane which ravaged Normandy just after Christmas, unforgettably marking the century's end and the mythic transition to the year 2000. The splendid pattern of the branches, the fountains, and the lawns has given way to a nightmare from which there is no waking, compared with which the historic damages — as they were called at the time — of that tornado of '87 previously described in my text seem trivial indeed. It will take months and months this time, if not years, merely to clear away the hundreds of giant tree trunks broken up into an inextricable tangle (crushing the young trees so lovingly cared for) and the enormous stumps torn out of the ground, leaving gaping holes, as though dug by the bombs of an incredible blitzkrieg lasting all of half an hour.

I have frequently mentioned the joyous creative energy which humanity must ceaselessly expend in order to restore the ruined world by means of new constructions. And so I am returning to that manuscript after a whole year of movie writing interspersed with all too many journeys, only a few days after the destruction of a notable part of my life, finding myself back in Berlin after another cataclysm, under another name, assigned a false occupation and carrying several false passports and performing an enigmatic mission always on the verge of collapsing, nevertheless continuing to struggle in the midst of doublings, ineffable apparitions, recurrent images in reiterating mirrors.

It is, at this moment, with a livelier gait that Wall continues on his way toward the end of our Feldmesserstrasse with its double quay, turning then quite noticeably in the direction of number 2, where the hypothetical doll shop for children and adults is located. The 1900-style ironwork gate is ajar, but the traveler dares not push it any farther open; he prefers to indicate his presence by pulling on a little chain hanging on the left side of the gate, thereby ringing a little bell, though its vigorous and repeated utilization does not produce any perceptible sound nor any human manifestation.

Then Wall looks up at the façade of the attractive villa, where the central window of the second floor is wide open. In the open recess appears a female person whom the visitor at first takes for a shop-window mannequin, so perfect from a distance does her immobility appear, the hypothesis of her being shown facing the street seeming moreover quite likely, given the commercial nature of the premises as announced on the signboard at the door. But suddenly receiving a brilliant glance of the eyes, which are fixed upon him, while a faint smile parts the lips in their pouting expression, Wall must acknowledge his mistake: despite the cold which she must be enduring in an outrageously flimsy garb, the doll—may God forgive me!—is a young girl of flesh and blood staring at him with ostentatious effrontery. The girl, with her rumpled blond curls, perhaps just getting out of bed, is, it must be said, very *mignonne*, insofar at least as this French adjective, with its connotations of charm and delicacy, might consort with her youthful beauty, her immodest posture, and her triumphant airs, which, on the contrary, suggest a determined, adventurous, even aggressive character, without the fragility her tender age (some thirteen or fourteen years) would normally suggest.

Since she hasn't deigned to reply to the vague nod he has just given her, Wall turns his eyes from the disturbing apparition, more or less abashed by this unexpected welcome. Hence it is with an even more emphatic determination that he deliberately pushes open the gate, crosses the narrow gar-

den, and makes for the stoop, mounting the three steps with
a firm stride. To the right of the door, against the brick jamb,
there is a round bronze bell, its nipple polished by visitors'
fingers, above the traditional plaque engraved with the name
"Joëlle Kast." Wall presses the button decisively.

After a long and silent moment of waiting, the heavy
carved wooden door is opened with — apparently — some
reluctance, and an old woman dressed in black appears in
the doorway. Before Boris Wallon has had time to introduce
himself or to formulate the slightest word of excuse, the
chaperone informs him in a low, confidential tone of voice
that the sale of dolls does not begin until afternoon, though
it continues through the evening, which, adding to the pre-
cociously erotic scene offered at the window of the upper
floor, reinforces in our out-of-bounds special agent the suspicions evoked earlier. He then utters the sentence he has just
prepared, in a correct but doubtless somewhat labored German, asking if Herr Dany von Brücke can receive him, although he has no fixed appointment with the man.

The ancient crone with the severe expression then opens
the door wider in order to get a better look at this traveling
salesman without a suitcase whose general aspect she regards
with a sort of incredulous amazement which gradually turns
into a distinct expression of terror, as if she were afraid she
was dealing with a madman. And she abruptly shuts the door,
its thick panel slamming closed with a loud thud. Just above,
out of sight, the shrill laughter of the invisible young girl,
whose image nonetheless persists, seized by a sudden gaiety
for some reason which escapes me, continues without re-

straint. The high-pitched peals are interrupted only to give way to an appealingly rich voice, uttering in French a mocking exclamation: *"Pas de chance pour aujourd'hui!"*

The rejected visitor leans backward, tilting his head: the brazen gamine is silhouetted against the sky, leaning forward over the railing, her transparent nightgown more than half-unbuttoned, as if, sleeping late, she had hastily begun taking off her doll's nightie to slip into something more proper. She shrieks: "Wait! I'll let you in!" But now her whole body, even less clothed than before (one shoulder and the meager bust are now revealed), appears in the empty space in an improbable, dangerous, desperate manner. Her eyes widen over glaucous depths. Her excessively red mouth opens too wide to utter a scream, which cannot be heard. Her slender torso, her bare arms, her head of blond curls twist and turn in all directions, struggling, writhing in a thousand increasingly excessive gesticulations. It seems as if she's calling for help, as if some imminent danger is threatening her—leaping flames, the vampire's sharp teeth, a murderer brandishing a knife—coming inexorably closer up in her bedroom. She is willing to risk everything to escape—actually she's already falling, an interminable fall, and she's already lying crushed on the gravel path of the little garden . . . when all of a sudden she withdraws, sucked back inside by the bedroom itself, and immediately vanishes.

Wall assumes his initial posture, facing the door, which is again partially open; but instead of the inhospitable chaperone, a young woman (of about thirty) is standing motionless in the open space, staring at the stranger, who indicates his surprise by an embarrassed smile. He stammers some incomprehensible excuses in German. But she continues staring at him in silence, her expression serious, doubtless friendly, though touched with a melancholy, remote sweetness, strongly contrasting with the cavalier exuberance of the adolescent girl at the window. And if the figures of the two seem to have some features in common—particularly the almond shape of the large green eyes, the prepossessing fleshy mouth, a straight delicate nose of the style known as Grecian, though more marked in the older of the two—the latter's dark brown hair is parted down the center in the fashion of the twenties, emphasizing a difference which is surely not merely that of the two generations. Her pupils move imperceptibly, as do her just-parted lips.

The seductive lady with the appealingly pursed lips and the faintly melancholy expression finally speaks, her voice warm and low, emanating from deep in her chest or even lower, her French flavored with the intonations of ripe cherries and fleshy apricots—sensual resonances, one might say in her case—noticed previously in the little girl: "Don't pay too much attention to Gigi, nor to what she says or might do. . . . The child's a little crazy, it's something to do with her age, she's just fourteen . . . and she has such unfortunate friends."

Then, after a more significant pause, while Wall is still hesitating about what he should say, she adds with the same almost absent deliberation: "Doctor von Brücke hasn't lived here for the last ten years. I'm so sorry. . . . My own name is over here. [With a graceful movement of her bare arm,

she indicates the bronze plaque above the bell.] But you can
call me Jo, it's simpler, though Germans pronounce it 'Io,'
pursued once by a gadfly across Greece and Asia Minor,
after Jupiter raped her in the form of a fiery-tinted cloud."

Joëlle Kast's smile, at this incongruous mythological
evocation, plunges the visitor into a labyrinth of dreamy suppositions. And therefore he ventures, almost at random:
"And what would there be to be sorry about, if I'm not being
indiscreet?"

"In the breakup with Daniel? [A throaty laugh suddenly animates the young woman, deep and cooing as if it
emanated from her entire body.] As far as I'm concerned,
nothing! No regrets! I was speaking in your behalf, on account of your investigation . . . Monsieur Wallon."

"Ah, you know who I am?"

"Pierre Garin told me you were coming. . . . [A silence]
Do come in! I'm getting cold out here."

Wall takes advantage of the long dark hallway through
which she leads him—to a sort of salon, also rather dark,
crowded with various pieces of furniture, huge decorative
dolls, and various more or less unexpected objects (such as
are found in junk shops)—to consider the turn his situation
has just taken. Has he fallen into another trap? Sitting on a
stiff red plush chair, its mahogany arms protected with
heavy ornamental bronze insets, he inquires, having opted
for the most natural tone of voice he can manage: "You know
Pierre Garin?"

"Of course!" she answers with a slightly weary shrug
of her shoulders. "Everyone here knows Pierre Garin. As

for Daniel, I was married to him for five years, just before
the war. . . . He was Gigi's father."

"Why do you say he 'was'?" the traveler asks, after a
moment's reflection.

The lady looks at him without answering, as if pondering the question, unless she's suddenly thought of something
entirely different, then finally announces in a neutral, indifferent tone of voice: "Gigi's an orphan. Colonel von Brücke
was murdered by Israeli agents two nights ago, in the Soviet zone . . . just opposite the apartment where my daughter and I lived, after my repudiation early in 1940."

"What do you mean by 'repudiation'?"

"Daniel had the right, or even the duty to do it. According to the new laws of the Reich I was Jewish, and he was
a high officer. For the same reason, he's never acknowledged
Gigi, who was born just before we got married."

"You speak French without a trace of a German or
Middle European accent. . . ."

"I was brought up in France and I am French. . . . But
at home we spoke a sort of Serbo-Croatian as well. My parents came from Klagenfurt. . . . 'Kast' is a distorted abbre-
viation of 'Kastanjevica,' a small town in Slovenia."

"And you stayed in Berlin all through the war?"

"You must be joking! My status became increasingly
risky, awkward for our everyday life. I scarcely dared leave
the house. . . . Daniel would visit us once a week. . . . Early
in the spring of '41 he managed to find a way for us to leave.
I still had my French passport. We settled in Nice, in the
Italian zone of occupation. *Oberführer* von Brücke left for

the Eastern front with his unit, in the strategic information services."

"He was a Nazi?"

"Probably, like everybody else. . . . I don't think the
question ever came up. As a German officer, he obeyed his
country's orders, and Germany was National Socialist. . . .
Actually, I don't know what he could have been doing
during our last interview, in Provence, until his return to
Berlin a few months ago. When the front was broken in
Mecklenburg after Admiral Dönetz's surrender, Daniel might
have joined his family at Stralsund, demobilized by the Rus-
sians as he was for obscure political reasons. For my part, I
came back here as soon as I could, with the French occupation forces. I speak English as easily as I do German and I
manage pretty well in Russian, which has a number of points
in common with Slovenian. I soon sent for Gigi, through the
Red Cross, and we got back without difficulty to our old house
on the canal, miraculously spared by the war. I had kept my
Berlin administrative papers proving that I would be recov-
ering my home here, and that Gigi herself was born here. A
nice American lieutenant managed to clear up the situation:
certificate of registration, ration cards, and all the rest. . . ."

The former Madame Joëlle von Brücke, née Kastanjevica, known as Kast ("Call me Jo, it's simpler"), presents
all these confidences with such an obvious concern for clarity, for coherence and precision, specifying each time the
places and the dates of her peregrinations without forgetting their quite justified motives, that Boris Robin, who had

asked for no such thing, cannot help finding her story suspicious if not highly unlikely. It was as if she were reciting a lesson carefully learned by heart, being careful to leave nothing out. And no doubt her reasonable, detached tone, without rancor or excitement, counts for a good deal in the insidious sensation of falseness which it inspires. Pierre Garin himself might have made up the whole of this edifying odyssey. To clear his conscience, he'll have to interrogate the eccentric adolescent, surely less carefully prepared than her mother. But why does the latter, who seems neither very expansive nor garrulous by nature, so insist on planting in a stranger's mind these tedious details concerning her family chronicle? What's being hidden by her inexplicable zeal, her niggling though defective memory (for all the apparent exhaustiveness of the narrative)? Why was she in such a hurry to get back to this strange city almost completely in ruins, difficult of access, perhaps still dangerous for her very life? Exactly what does she know about von Brücke's death? Did she have an essential part to play in it? Or just a walk-on role? What riddle is the J.K. apartment the heart of? How can she be so sure of the specific scene of the crime? And how, on the other hand, can Pierre Garin have guessed that the traveler has chosen, at the last moment, the one passport made out to the name of Wallon for use in the city's western zone? Was Maria, the charming servant in the Hôtel des Alliés, let in on the secret? And finally, what means of existence did the so-called Jo have all this time in Berlin, where she immediately sent for her underage daughter, who of course would have continued her studies more easily in a school in Nice or Cannes?[7]

    7. The various questions our anxious narrator pretends to be asking himself with a pseudo-naiveté allow him to commit at least one mistake in the complicated arrangement of his pawns: he admits incidentally that he suspects the precious Maria—and not the Mahler twins—of working for the DAS, whereas that morning she didn't even understand our language. Stranger still, on his part, he confuses the single interrogation which strikes us as pertinent (strikes me in particular) and which concerns him directly: would not the disenchanted young widow remind him of another feminine presence, eternally hovering over his narrative and touching him very closely? Doesn't the description he gives of her face, with its firm features, seem to relate directly to a photograph of his own mother when the latter was thirty, an image to which he has frequently alluded? Yet he carefully avoids any mention of a resemblance, however incontestable (accentuated further by the affecting sonority of the voice which he has described elsewhere), while he profits by the slightest occasion, throughout his text, to indicate the possibly imaginary similarities or duplications—unconvincing in any case and considerably removed from one another in time. On the other hand, he insists quite freely (and in a doubtless premeditated fashion) on the sexual aura of Jo Kast as well as of the scandalous adolescent with golden curls, though the morphological comparison he establishes between mother and daughter strikes us, once more, as quite subjective, not to say marked by a mendacious intention.

    Dany von Brücke's "natural" daughter is much more likely to be the image of the "Aryan" beauty of her male progenitor who, while denying her his noble ancestral title, has nonetheless decked her out in an archaic and virtually extinct Prussian given name: Gegenecke, swiftly transformed into Gege—i.e., Guégué according to the German pronunciation, but Gallicized as Gigi and then turned into Djidji for the Americans. In passing I remark, for those who might not yet have understood, that this capricious young creature, so remarkable for her precocity in several realms, is one of the chief agents of our tactical forces.

Pondering these mysteries, Wall, whose eyes have now grown accustomed to the dim light, which makes the large salon—with its heavy red curtains drawn almost completely across the windows—so obscure, inspects more closely its decoration of some oneiric flea market, an oppressive attic, or a shop of buried souvenirs, where the presence, among the more or less miniaturized children's toys, of numerous life-size dolls with suggestive accoutrements, contrasting with their juvenile expressions, would be likely to suggest some 1900s brothel much more than a toy shop for little girls. And the visitor's imagination speculates once again concerning the kind of enterprise carried on in this venerable middle-class residence of an officer of the Wehrmacht.

Emerging finally from his reverie (after how long an interval?), the traveler brings his eyes back to the lady. . . . He realizes with some surprise that the armchair in which she was sitting a few moments before is now empty. And, turning in his seat, he fails to find her in any other point of the huge room. The hostess would thus have left the salon with its erotic dolls and abandoned her visitor without allowing him to detect any sound of her footsteps or the slightest creak of the parquet floor or a grating of a door hinge. Why has she suddenly left the room so secretly? Might she have run to tell Pierre Garin that the migratory bird is now caught in the meshes of his net? Would the DAS men already be there in the villa, where an alarming disturbance is audible upstairs? But now at this very moment the ineffable widow with green eyes, assuaged by mendacious languors, discreetly returns to the salon/shop by some imperceptible entrance, located somewhere in the depths of a room so dark that the young woman seems to be emerging out of the shadows, carefully carrying a saucer with a brimming cup which she is being careful not to spill. While keeping a watchful eye on the level of the liquid, she approaches with a dancer's immaterial step, saying: "I've fixed you a cup of coffee, Monsieur Wallon, nice and strong, the way the Italians make it. . . . A little bitter, but still, I'm sure you've never tasted anything nearly so good in the Communist zone. Here, thanks to the United States Quartermaster Corps, we have the advantage of certain hard-to-get products. [She puts her precious gift between his hands.] It's *robusta* from Colombia. . . ." And after a silence, while he begins to sip the scorching black infusion, she adds in a more intimate, maternal tone of voice: "You're so tired, my poor Boris, that you went to sleep while I was talking!"

The drink is indeed so strong that it's a little nauseating; it's certainly not what's called a *café américain*. . . . Having nonetheless managed to swallow it, the traveler feels no better—rather, the contrary. In order to stem his growing nausea, he gets up from his chair, leaving his empty cup on the marble top of an end table already overloaded with small objects: purses of metallic mesh, flowers made of beads, hat pins, mother-of-pearl boxes, exotic seashells . . . in front of several family photographs of various sizes, clustered diagonally in perforated brass frames. In the center, the largest of these shows a vacation scene at the seashore, with great rounded boulders on the left side, and far in the background, glistening little waves; in front of all this, four persons are standing on the sand, lined up facing the camera.

The shot might just as well have been taken on a little Breton beach around León.

The two central figures of this image share the same Nordic blondness: a tall thin man with a handsome, severe face, at least fifty years old, wearing impeccable white trousers and a close-fitting white shirt buttoned up to the neck, and to his right a very little girl of perhaps a year and a half, two at the most, smiling winsomely, completely naked.

On each side of this pair—that is, at each end of the row—are standing two persons remarkable for their black heads of hair: a very pretty woman (of about twenty) who is holding a child by the hand and, on the other side, a man of thirty or thirty-five. Both are wearing black bathing suits (or at least dark enough to look black in a black-and-white photograph), covering the entire body in the first instance, but only the lower half of the body in the second, both persons still wet, apparently from a recent dip. Judging by their ages, these two very brown adults must be the parents of the little girl with wheat-colored curls, who has apprently received her grandfather's pale pigmentation as a Mendelian inheritance.

The latter, for the moment, is staring up, toward the edge of the shiny rectangle, at a flight of seabirds—shrieking gulls, black-headed terns, petrels returning to the open sea—or else at planes that are passing overhead outside the field of vision. The younger man is watching the little girl, who in her left hand is offering the photographer one of those tiny crabs, called "green crabs," so common on these beaches, which she is holding between two fingers by a hind leg, studying her catch with an amazed expression. Only the young mother Anadyomene is looking in the direction of the camera, posing with a lovely smile for the occasion. But, attracting more attention, clearly visible at the center of the image, the crab's two wide-open pincers and eight slender legs are spread out in a stiff fan, quite regularly spaced and perfectly symmetrical.

In order to study more closely the different actors of this complex scene, Wall has taken the frame in both hands and brought it closer to his eyes, as if he wanted to get inside it. He seems to be on the point of jumping in when his hostess's disturbing voice intervenes to pull him back at the last moment, murmuring just behind his ear: "That's Gigi at two, in a sandy creek on the northeast side of Rügen in the summer of '37, when it was unusually hot."

"And the glorious young woman holding her hand, whose shoulders and arms are still dripping seawater?"

"That's not the ocean, only the Baltic. And it's me, of course! [She greets the compliment by a little throaty laugh which vanishes as it breaks gently on the wet sand.] But I'd already been married a long time when that was taken."

"To the man who's also just come out of the water?"

"No, no! To Daniel, the chic gentleman, the much older one who could so easily be my father."

"Excuse me! [The polite visitor had of course recognized with no difficulty the old colonel in his statuesque pose from an allegorical statue back in the square in Berlin.] Why is he looking up into the sky?"

"There was some hellish noise from a Stuka patrol — I think it was a training flight."

"Did that have something to do with him?"

"I don't know. But the war was coming."

"He was very handsome."

"Wasn't he? A perfect specimen of a dolichocephalic blond for the zoo."

"Who took the photograph?"

"I don't remember. . . . Probably a professional, given the remarkable quality of the shot — all those tiny details; you could almost count the grains of sand. . . . As for the man with black hair on the far right, he's the son Dan had from his first marriage . . . to abide by the convenient expression. I don't think they were ever really married. . . ."

"An early affair, according to what seems the son's maturity?"

"Dan was no more than twenty, and his 'fiancée' barely eighteen, my age exactly when I first met him myself. . . . He's always had a great success with romantic girls. . . . Funny the way history repeats itself: she was French too, and according to the portraits I've managed to see, she looked like my twin sister, at thirty years' distance . . . or maybe a little more. You could say that he had very well-established sexual tastes! But that first involvement lasted much longer than ours. 'It was only a rehearsal,' he used to reassure me, 'before opening night.' I've gradually come to understand, on the contrary, that I must have been only a repetition . . . or at best the star of some sort of ephemeral reprise of an old play. . . . But what's the matter, my dear man? You seem even more exhausted than you were. You can hardly stand up — please sit down! . . ."

Wallon was now feeling really ill, as though under the
effect of some drug, the bitter taste of which persisted in his
mouth in a disturbing manner, while the mistress of the
house suddenly brought her explanations and commentaries to an end, the suddenly piercing gaze of her green eyes
examining her captive as he turned and staggered toward
the salon in search of a place to sit down. . . .[8]

8. Taking advantage of the situation in which our troubled agent
is drowning in the flood of imperfect and past tenses, we can clarify or
correct certain points of detail in the preceding dialogue. If my memory
serves, the family-vacation photo was not taken on the island of Rügen,
but in the immediate environs of Graal-Mürutz, a Baltic seaside resort
closer to Rostock, where Franz Kafka stayed during the summer of 1923
(that is, fourteen years earlier) before coming to spend his last winter
in Berlin, not moreover in the center of town, as our narrator has supposed above, but in the fringe neighborhood of Steglitz, which today,
with Tempelhof, marks the southern limit of the American zone.

   And I also recall the planes in the sky, for it was not indeed a flight
of the ash-colored cranes, so spectacular at that season, which the father
was observing. Yet it was not, on the other hand, the Stukas in a training
flight, but the Messerschmitt 109s roaring at high altitude, without much
disturbing the summer people's repose. Joëlle Kastanjevica's mistake
derives from a confusion with the remarkable war-propaganda film we
had seen that same day in the newsreels, in a primitive Ribnitz-Damgarten
movie theater. As for the vocabulary of theater people which she uses
concerning her marriage ("rehearsal," "opening night," "reprise," etc.) its
obvious origin was her stay in Nice (thus, much later). She ran a modest
neighborhood stationery shop there, where children came to buy pencils
and erasers, though she was much more interested in the troupe of amateur
actors some friends had founded. They say she distinguished herself in

All the armchairs were unfortunately occupied, not by
life-size dolls, as he had originally supposed, but by real adolescent girls in scanty underclothes who kept making funny
faces and winking conspiratorially. . . . In his bewilderment,
he dropped the gilded frame, and the glass smashed to pieces
on the floor with a disproportionately loud cymbal crash. . . .
Wall, suddenly imagining himself to be in danger, stepped
back toward the marble-topped end table, where he blindly
grabbed, behind his back, a small, rounded, smooth object,
like a polished pebble, which he thought would be heavy
enough to serve as a weapon of defense if he needed one. . . .
In front of him, Gigi was there, of course, sitting in the first
row, smiling at him with an expression both provocative and
derisive. Her companions, scattered around the room, also
accentuated for the Frenchman's benefit their lascivious attitudes. Sitting, standing, or half-reclining, several of them
seemed to be miming the living reproduction of more or
less famous works of art: Greuze's *Broken Pitcher* (but in a
further state of undress), Edouard Manneret's *Bait*, Fernand
Cormon's *Chained Captive*, Alice Liddell as a little beggar girl
with her shift in suggestive tatters photographed by the Ox-
ford don Charles Dodgson, Saint Agatha exposing her naked
breasts, already decorated with a very becoming wound under
the fair martyr's crown. . . . Wall opened his mouth to say

the role of Cordelia in a stage adaptation of *The Diary of a Seducer*, the
French translation having been published before the war in *Le Cabinet
cosmopolite*.

something, he didn't know what, which would save him from
the absurdity of his situation, or perhaps merely to utter a cry
as people do in nightmares, but no sound emerged from his
throat. Then he realized that in his right hand he was holding an enormous glass eye which must have come from
some giant doll, and he raised it to his own horrified eyes in
order to examine it more closely. . . . The girls all burst out
laughing at once, in their various timbres and registers, with
crescendos, shrill notes, and deeper trills, in a devastating
concert. . . .[9]

The traveler's last sensation was that he was being transported, weak and helpless as a rag doll, while the whole
house was filled with the racket of a chaotic shifting of fur-

9. The author of the problematic narrative doubtless seeks, by
his outrageous statements, to convince his eventual reader of the poi-
soning theory: hence we would be observing in this obviously delirious scene the first effects (nausea, then hallucinations) of the so-called
narcotic coffee we so carefully prepared. His plausible tactic, in the bad
pass from which he is struggling to escape, would thus be to dissolve
his personal responsibilities—conscious or unconscious, deliberate or
involuntary—in an opaque bath of complicated machinations hatched
by his adversaries, of false-bottomed drawers, of spells and various
hypnotic charms worked upon him, exonerating his unfortunate and
fragile person from any fault or implication. Obviously it would be
preferable if he himself could specify our own interest in destroying
him. Anyone who has examined his previous reports, however summarily or partially, will in any case be in a position to observe that these
twin themes of conspiracy and enchantment recur, under his pen, with
remarkable frequency, including the tumultuous final aggression by an
outburst of erotic little girls.

niture, or even of some kind of pillage, in what seemed the uproar of a riot.

Suddenly everything grew still. And it was in a total, too perfect, and rather disturbing silence that Franck Matthieu (or else Mathieu Frank, since what is involved are his two given names) awakens, at the end of an unknown number of hours, in a familiar bedroom of which he seems to recognize every last detail, though this setting is for the moment impossible to situate in space or time. It is night. The thick double curtains are drawn. Hanging in the center of the wall opposite the invisible window, there is the picture.

The walls are covered with an old-fashioned wallpaper with alternating vertical bands—rather dark bluish stripes with white edges, five or six centimeters wide—which leave equivalent but much paler surfaces between them, through which runs from top to bottom a line of tiny identical designs whose dull color must have originally been gilded. Without needing to stand up in order to see it at closer range, Mathieu F. can describe from memory this sign with its uncertain signification: a rosette, a sort of clove or a tiny torch, or else a dagger, but also a tiny doll whose body and two legs pressed together would replace the broad blade of the dagger or the handle of the torch, her head becoming either the latter's flame or the former's rounded handle, while the arms stretching forward (and thus slightly foreshortened) represented the hilt of the weapon or the cupel which keeps the burning substances from running onto the hand holding the torch.

Against the wall on the right (for the observer with his back to the window) stands a huge mirrored armoire, deep enough to hang clothes in, the heavy mirror with beveled edges occupying almost the whole of the single door, in which can be seen the image of the picture, but inverted—i.e., the right part of the wallpaper appearing in the left half of the re-flecting surface, and, reciprocally, the exact middle of the rectangular frame (materialized by the old man's nobly borne head) coinciding exactly with the central point of the pivot-ing mirror, which is closed and hence perpendicular to the real picture, and hence moreover to its virtual duplication.

On this same wall, between the armoire—placed almost in the corner—and the outside wall where the window is located, though it is entirely concealed by the drawn heavy curtains, are backed up the headboards of the twin beds, which are so narrow as not to be usable except by very young children: less than one and a half meters in length by about seventy centimeters in width. They are separated from each other by a painted wooden night table of matching di-mensions, which holds a small lamp in the form of a candle-stick, its faint electric bulb not turned off. The second night table, absolutely identical to the first, being the same pale blue color and holding the same lit lamp, finds just the space it requires between the second bed and the outside wall, im-mediately next to the left edge of the ample folds created by the dark red material of which the curtains are made. These must considerably overlap the invisible window recess, which would have little reason to be a bay wider than the kind built nowadays.

Wanting to check a detail to which he has not had ac-cess in his prone position, Mathieu props himself up on one elbow. The two pillows are each embroidered, as might be expected, with the initial of a given name in large gothic capital letters in high relief, and in them can be readily recognized, notwithstanding the highly ornamented complication of the three parallel legs which each of them involves, not at first glance easily differentiated from each other, the letter M and the letter W. It is at this moment that the traveler understands how bizarre his situation is: he is lying stretched out in pajamas, his head supported by a sort of heavy linen bolster propped against the wall beneath the window, on a mattress without a sheet lying on the floor between the foot of the twin beds and the long toilet table, on the white marble top of which rest two identical porcelain bowls, though one has a clearly visible crack blackened by time and repaired by means of metal clasps now corroded by rust. In the decoration of monochrome flowered volutes which embellishes a squat water pitcher, placed between the two bowls and made of the same material, appears a large escutcheon on which can be read with some difficulty the same two quite similar gothic letters, this time so ingeniously interlaced that only an experienced eye can permit them to be identified.

The neck of the pitcher is reflected in one of the twin mirrors attached to the striped wallpaper, over each bowl at a height suitable only for very young boys. The same is the case for the level of the white marble tabletop. In the other mirror (the one on the right) appears once again an image of the picture, its design inverted. But in observing the first (the one on the left) more closely, a third reproduction can be discovered, distinctly farther away, of the same picture, with its design, in this case, the right way round — that is, reflected (and inverted) twice over: first of all in the toilet-table mirror, then in the mirror of the armoire door.

Mathieu struggles to his feet, his whole body exhausted for some unknown reason, and goes over to look at his unshaven face by leaning toward the middle of the little mirror over the mended bowl, the one involving in the design painted inside it a big letter M, barred diagonally by the old crack in the porcelain. The picture represents some episode (perhaps quite famous, but he has always wondered which one) of ancient history or of mythology, in a hilly landscape in which can be made out in the distance, to the left, several columned buildings in Corinthian style forming the background of the setting. Coming from the right, in the foreground, a horseman riding his black stallion brandishes a warlike sword in the direction of the old man in a toga who is facing him, standing in a high-wheeled chariot which he stops in its course, restraining by their taut reins the two white horses, one of which, more nervous than the other, rears and whinnies, suffering from the bit, which is too suddenly tightened.

Behind this proud driver of such august stature, who is crowned with a royal diadem, stand two archers in rigid loincloths who stretch their bows, but without the arrows seeming to be pointed toward the untimely aggressor, whom they do not even appear to notice. The latter wears a pectoral cuirass which might well be Roman, and its probably from another period than the vaguely Hellenic toga of the old king, whose one bared shoulder has nothing bellicose about it, while the short fitted loincloths of the two soldiers, as well as the headgear extending very low on the napes of their necks and over their ears, suggests something rather Egyptian. But one detail is even more disturbing from the historical point of view: among the stones in the road lies a woman's shoe, a delicate high-heeled dancing slipper, its triangular vamp covered with blue sequins sparkling in the sun.

The immemorial scene transpires once more, in its familiar strangeness. Mathieu pours a little water in his bowl, the glued crack being much more noticeable than it used to be. How long has it been since this yellowish liquid has been renewed? Unconsciously making the gestures of his childhood, he immerses the washcloth bearing the letters M v B, sewn in red thread on the narrow hem which serves to hang the cloth on the hooked end of the chromium-plated brass towel rack. M rubs his face gingerly with the dripping, spongy material. This is not sufficient, unfortunately, to reduce the nausea which has overcome him ever more powerfully. His head is swimming; his legs collapse. Pushed back against the wall, on the left side of the picture, the mannequin is still there. . . . Lifting his toothbrush glass, he drinks a mouthful of lukewarm water that tastes like ashes and immediately lets himself fall back onto the mattress.

Third Day

HR awakens in an unknown bedroom which must be a children's room, given the miniature size of the twin beds, the night tables, the toilet table with its double complement of thick porcelain bowls painted with a grayish design. He himself is lying on a bare mattress, though of adult dimensions, placed directly on the floor. There is also a big traditional mirrored armoire, its heavy door ajar, looking gigantic in this room of doll furniture. Over his head, the electric light is on: a cup-shaped translucent ceiling fixture representing a woman's face completely surrounded by long undulating serpentine locks, like a sun's rays. But so bright is the harsh light that he cannot explore the details any further. On the striped wallpaper facing his mattress hangs an academic painting, a vague imitation of Delacroix or Géricault, with nothing remarkable about it save its huge size and mediocre quality.

In the big beveled mirror of the armoire appears the reflection of the wide-open bedroom door. In the doorway, and against the dark background of the hallway, stands Gigi, staring at the traveler lying on his mattress. Since he habitually sleeps on his right side, he sees the girl only by means of her reflection in the armoire mirror—twice removed, it would seem, in a very calculated fashion. Yet the young visitor is staring directly at the bottom of the red curtains and the bolster, without glancing at the armoire mirror, so that she cannot know if the sleeper has his eyes open now, watching her, and speculating further about this strange child. Why does this active little creature remain silent and motionless, keeping watch so attentively over the guest's troubling repose? Is there something abnormal about such sleep; is it too sound, is it lasting too long? Has some physician, summoned by an emergency call, already attempted to rouse the man? Is there a sort of anguish to be discerned on the child's pretty face?

The evocation of a doctor possibly being at his bedside suddenly wakens in HR's troubled mind a fragile and fragmentary memory from his immediate past. A man with a bald skull, a Lenin goatee, and steel-rimmed glasses, holding a notepad and pen, was sitting on a chair at the foot of the mattress, while he himself, his eyes on the ceiling, talked on and on, but in a hoarse, unrecognizable voice, without managing to control what he was saying. What could he be telling in his delirium? Now and then he cast a terrified glance at his impassive examiner, behind whom was standing another man, smiling for no evident reason. And this latter man curiously resembled HR himself, the more so because he had put on the suit and the fur-lined jacket in which the special agent had arrived in Berlin.

And now this false HR, whose face remained quite identifiable despite his obviously artificial mustache, has leaned toward the recording physician to whisper something in his ear, while showing him a passage in a bundle of manuscript pages. . . . The image freezes for a few seconds in the incontestable density of the real, and then collapses with disconcerting speed. Scarcely a minute later, the whole phantasmal sequence has vanished, dissolved in the mist, completely unreal. Doubtless there was nothing more to it than the drifting residue of a dream fragment.

Today Gigi is wearing a navy-blue schoolgirl's dress, pretty enough though reminiscent of the severe costume of religious boarding schools with its short pleated skirt, its white socks, and its demure white collar. And now she's moving quite decisively, though gracefully too, toward the mirrored armoire, as if she had just discovered its inopportune (or else henceforth useless) opening. With a careful gesture she closes the door, its rusty hinges creaking for several seconds. HR pretends to waken with a start because of the noise; he hurriedly readjusts the buttons of the pajamas that someone has put on him (who? when? why?) and abruptly sits up. As casually as possible, despite a persistent uncertainty about just where he is and the reasons that have led to his sleeping here, he says: "Hello, little girl!"

The child responds by no more than a toss of her head. She seems preoccupied, perhaps upset. As a matter of fact, her behavior is so different from that of the day before (but was it the day before?) that she might be an altogether different girl, though physically identical with the first one. The bewildered traveler risks a neutral question, offered in an indifferent tone of voice: "Are you off to school, dear?"

"No, why?" she asks in a sulky, surprised tone of voice. "I've been through with my courses and homework and tests for a long time. . . . Besides, you don't have to call me 'dear.'"

"Whatever you like. . . . I guess I was influenced by what you're wearing."

"What's that got to do with it? These are my working clothes. Besides, no one goes to school in the middle of the night."

While Gigi stares at herself in the armoire mirror, methodically passing her entire person in review, from the blond curls she ruffles quite knowingly to the white socks she pushes a little farther down on her ankles, HR, as if such scrutiny were contagious, stands up to inspect his own exhausted face, bending far over toward one of the two toilet mirrors, placed too low for easy examination, above the porcelain bowls. His borrowed sky-blue striped pajamas have the letter W embroidered on the left breast pocket. Without seeming to attach much importance to the question, he asks: "What kind of work?"

"Dance hostess."

"At your age? In that dress?"

"There's no particular age for work like that, as you ought to know, Monsieur Frenchman. As far as the dress goes, it's compulsory in the cabaret where I'm a waitress, among other things. . . . It reminds the German officers of their absent families!"

HR has turned toward the promising nymph, who takes advantage of this movement to emphasize the irony of her observation by a naughty wink, behind a lock of hair that has fallen over one eyelid and her cheek. Her indecent gesture seems all the more suggestive in that the young lady has tucked up to her waist her full skirt, with its carefully pressed pleats, in order to adjust in front of the mirror her rather too loose panties, being careful not to let the appropriate gaps disappear. Her bare legs are smooth and suntanned all the way to the top of her thighs, as if this were still high summer at the beach. He asks: "Who's this W whose pajamas I'm wearing?"

"Walther, of course!"

"And who's Walther?"

"Walther von Brücke, my half-brother. You saw him yesterday in the vacation photograph, the one at the seashore in the salon downstairs."

"Does he live here?"

"Of course not! Thank God! The house had been empty and closed for a long time when Io moved in, at the end of '46. That donkey Walther had to get himself killed as a hero on the Russian front during the German retreat. Or else he's rotting in a camp somewhere in the wilds of Siberia."[10]

Gigi, who has meanwhile reopened the creaking door of the big armoire, only half of which is fitted out as a closet, now searches frantically among the clothes, lingerie, and trinkets heaped up in great confusion on the shelves, apparently looking for some little object she fails to find. A belt? A handkerchief? A piece of costume jewelry? In her exasperation she drops on the floor a delicate high-heeled black slipper whose triangular vamp is entirely covered with blue sequins. HR asks if she has lost something, but she doesn't bother to reply. Yet she must have laid her hand on what she was looking for, some very discreet accessory of an unimaginable nature, for when she closes the armoire again and turns back toward him it is with, quite suddenly, her first smile. He asks: "If I'm not mistaken, I'm using your room?"

"No, not really. You saw the size of the beds! But it's the only mirror in the house where you can see yourself from head to toe. . . . Besides, it used to be my room, in the old days . . . practically from birth, until 1940. . . . I was five. I used to play I was two people, because of the two beds and the two bowls. Some days I was W, and others I was M. Though they were twins, they must have been quite different from each other. I made up special habits for each of

---

10. Unpleasant to her colleagues whenever she has the chance, our budding trollop employs her customary effrontery here. And merely for the gratuitous pleasure of lying, for no Service directive provided this absurd detail, all too easy to refute.

them, and very marked characters, personal peculiarities, notions, and ways of behaving that were totally opposed to each other. . . . I was careful to respect the imaginary identity of each one."

"What's become of M?"

"Nothing. Markus von Brücke died when he was very young. . . . Would you like me to open the curtains?"

"Why bother. Didn't you say it was a dark night?"

"It doesn't matter. You'll see! There's no window anyway. . . ."

Having regained her juvenile exuberance for no obvious reason, the girl takes three elastic leaps over the blue-striped mattress, crossing the space separating the mirrored armoire from the closely drawn curtains, which she slides with both hands in opposite directions across their gilded metal rod, the wooden rings dividing the curtains right and left with a loud clicking noise, as though to make room, in their median separation, for the expected stage of a theater. But behind the heavy curtains there is nothing but the wall.

This wall, as a matter of fact, contains no sort of bay or window in the old style, nor the slightest opening of any kind, except in trompe l'oeil: a painted window frame looking out on an imaginary exterior, both painted on the plaster with an amazing effect of tangible presence, accentuated by tiny spotlights ingeniously arranged so that the gesture of opening the curtains must have turned them on. Framed by a classic French window, the wood of which was represented with hypertrophic realism, the molding showing every last scratch or defect in the grain, its iron bolt rusted in places, and beyond the twelve rectangular panes (two rows of three in each "door") appears a ruined landscape of war. Dead or dying men lie here and there among the rubble, wearing the greenish, easily identifiable uniforms of the Wehrmacht. Most have lost their helmets. A column of disarmed prisoners, in the same more or less ragged and filthy uniforms, vanishes into the distance to the right, guarded by Russian soldiers covering them with the short barrels of their automatic assault rifles.

In the foreground, life-size and so close that he seems two steps away from the house, staggers a wounded noncommissioned officer, also a German, blinded by a hastily improvised bandage around his head from ear to ear, stained red over his eyes. Moreover, some blood has trickled under this bandage and around his nostrils down to his mustache. His right hand, held out in front of his face, fingers spread wide, seems to beat the air ahead of him for fear of some possible obstacle. And yet a blond girl of thirteen or fourteen, dressed like a little Ukrainian or Bulgarian peasant, is holding his left hand to guide him, or more precisely to pull him toward that improbable and providential window which she has been struggling to reach since the beginning of time, her free (left) hand extended toward the miraculously intact panes, where she is about to knock in the hope of finding some help, some refuge in any case, not so much for herself as for this blind man she has taken charge of, God knows with what obscure intentions. . . . Upon closer consideration, it appears that this charitable child distinctly resembles Gigi. In her exertions, she has lost the bright-colored cloth which

in normal circumstances would cover her head. The golden
locks flutter around her head, her features excited by this bold
course through unknown perils. . . . After a long silence,
she murmurs in an incredulous tone of voice, as if she can
scarcely admit the existence of the picture:

"It must have been Walther who painted that crazy
thing, to take his mind off . . . everything."

"And there was no real window in the children's room?"

"Yes, of course there was! . . . Overlooking the back
garden, there were even some big trees . . . and goats. It must
have been walled up later, for unknown reasons, probably
at the very beginning of the siege of Berlin. Io says the mural
was painted during the final battle by my half-brother, who
was caught here on his last leave."[11]

11. The unpredictable Guégué, for once in her life, is not making
something up but accurately reporting some correct information furnished by her mother. Except for one detail: I had not reached the banks
of the Spree on leave, which would scarcely have been conceivable in the
spring of '45, but on the contrary on a highly dangerous "special contact
mission," which the Russo-Polish offensive, launched on April 22, immediately rendered null and void. Unfortunately or fortunately, who can
ever say? Note as well — and it is anything but surprising — that the girl
doesn't seem at all concerned about a certain incoherence in her remarks:
if I am in Berlin during the final assault, I can hardly be dead a few months
earlier, during rearguard skirmishes in the Ukraine, Byelorussia, or Po-
land, as she appeared to believe likely a few moments earlier.

As for the presence of Greek ruins on the distant hills remarked
by the narrator, this was merely — if I remember correctly — a sort of
mirror image of those already appearing in the big allegorical scene
which, from my earliest childhood, hung on the opposite wall of this

HR, still lost in his contemplation of the enigmatic mural which substitutes for a window in the children's room where he has slept, particularly fascinated by that life-size adolescent girl who knocks at the windowpane (also in trompe l'oeil) to ask for help, so present—not only by her

---

children's room. It might also be a reference, though, or an unconscious homage to the painter Lovis Corinth, whose work once had a strong influence on my own, almost as much, I suspect, as that of Caspar David Friedrich, who struggled all his life on the island of Rügen to express what David d'Angers calls "the tragedy of landscape." But the style adopted for the mural in question doesn't have much to do with either one, except maybe for the latter's dramatic skies; what mattered for me was to portray in the minutest detail an authentic and personal image of war, directly from the front.

Reference to my beloved Friedrich leads me to correct an incomprehensible error (unless, once again, this was an intentional falsification for an obscure motive) committed by the so-called Henri Robin concerning the geological nature of the soil on the German coast of the Baltic. Caspar David Friedrich, as a matter of fact, has produced countless canvases representing the sparkling marble, or more prosaically the luminous white chalk cliffs which have made Rügen so famous. That our scrupulous chronicler should have retained the memory of enormous blocks of granite, resembling the Armorican boulders of his childhood, quite bewilders me, the more so since his solid agronomist's training, which he deliberately mentions (or even parades, some say), should have kept him from falling into this unlikely confusion; in this northern region, the old Hercynian shelf never extends beyond the overwhelming Harz massif, where moreover so many Celtic and Germanic legends are to be met with: the magical forest of the Perthes, which is another Brocéliande, and the young witches of the *Walpurgisnacht*.

Among these, the one who concerns us now, and whom we designate in our messages by the code name GG (or else 2G), might be

outstretched hand, but especially by her angelic face, rosy with emotion; her wide green eyes, wider still with the excitement of the adventure; her mouth, with its fleshy lips just parted and on the point of uttering a long cry of distress — and so near that she seems to have already entered the room,

---

the worst kind, one of the unreal legion of barely nubile flower maidens in the power of the Arthuro-Wagnerian wizard Klingsor. While attempting to keep her under control, I must for the sake of the cause pretend to submit to her almost daily extravagances and indulge her in whims of which I might gradually become the accomplice, without being entirely conscious of a spell which would inexorably lead me to a perhaps imminent death . . . or worse still, to loss of willpower and madness. . . .

Already I wonder if it is really an accident that she happened to be on my path. I was prowling that day around Father's house, where I had not set foot since the surrender. I knew that Dany had returned to Berlin but was staying somewhere else, probably in the Russian zone, more or less clandestinely, and that Jo, his second wife, whom he had to repudiate in 1940, had just taken up residence on the premises with the blessing of the American Secret Service. Rigged out with a false mustache and big dark glasses, which on principle I wear on days that are too bright (to protect my eyes, still delicate ever since my wound of October '44 in Transylvania), with a broad-brimmed hat pulled down over my forehead, I ran no risk of being recognized by my young mother-in-law (she's fifteen years younger than I), if she had taken it into her head to come outside at that very moment. Standing in front of the open door, I pretended to be interested in the varnished wood panel of recent manufacture, decorated with elegant hand-painted scrollwork meant to reproduce the 1900-type hardware that constituted the old fence, as if I just happened to be looking for dolls, or else had some to sell, a supposition which would not, in a sense, have been entirely mistaken.

Then, looking up toward the still-appealing family villa, I was astonished to discover (how could I have failed to notice it when I arthen gives a start in hearing behind him the crystalline sound of breaking glass.

He quickly turns toward the opposite wall. In the left corner of the room, Gigi stands in the open doorway, still dressed in her schoolgirl outfit with its white lace collar,

---

rived?) that just above the door, with its high rectangular spy hole, its glass protected by massive cast-iron arabesques, the central window upstairs was wide open, which was hardly unusual in this warm autumn day. In the open space was standing a feminine figure which at first I took for a shop-window mannequin, so perfect did her immobility seem, at that distance, the hypothesis of such a display, boldly facing the street, seeming moreover quite likely, given the commercial nature of the premises advertised on the wooden panel serving as a signboard. As for the type of life-size doll selected to lure the customer (a slender adolescent girl with blond curls in suggestive disarray, presented in an outrageously transparent outfit, permitting, no, insisting on the attraction of her promising girlish charms), it could only reinforce the equivocal—not to say prostitutional—character of the handwritten sign, the traffic in minors for sexual purposes likely to be, in today's ruined Berlin, much more widespread than that of children's toys or wax figures for fashionable shops.

After carefully verifying one lexical detail referring to the sign's possible implications, I looked up toward the second floor. . . . The image had changed. It was no longer an erotic effigy from some wax museum whose budding attractions were exhibited at the window, but indeed a very young girl, very much alive, wriggling there in a fashion as excessive as it was incomprehensible, leaning forward over the railing with her transparent slip clinging now to just one shoulder, the already-loosened straps gradually coming undone. Yet even her most extreme gestures and attitudes retained a strange grace which suggested some delirious Cambodian Apsaras undulating her six arms in all directions, her slender waist rippling as delicately as her swanlike neck. Her reddish gold head of hair, illuminated by the afternoon sun, flamed around

looking down at her feet, where the sparkling debris resembles the remains of a champagne glass broken into hundreds of scattered fragments. The largest of these—and the
most recognizable—is connected to the stem and part of the
foot, no longer supporting anything more than a crystal

---

an angelic countenance of sensual curves, giving off sparks like a young
dragon hatching from her chrysalis.

The scene which follows this first apparition remains, even today,
tender and affecting in my memory. It was two days later, at nightfall.
Since I was not troubled by legalistic issues in those actually not so remote days, nor even with saving appearances, the organization of anti-
Nazi pseudo-resistants I belonged to at the time being nothing more, it
must be admitted, than a criminal mafia (pimping, selling bad drugs,
forging documents, ransoming former dignitaries of the fallen regime,
etc.) that flourished in the shadow of the NKVD, which we supplied
with all sorts of precious information, not counting our substantial assistance for particularly dangerous violent actions in the Western sec-
tors, I quite simply had the interesting nymph kidnapped, in order to
examine her in greater comfort, by three Yugoslav thugs, former de-
ported workers left to their own devices since the collapse of the regime and the closing of the war factories.

So she finds herself transported to our Treptow headquarters,
near the park but in an odd zone of abandoned warehouses and ruined
offices, between a railroad freight yard and the river. Despite the blockade, crossing the demarcation lines was no problem for us, even when
our luggage included a cumbersome trunk (containing an adolescent
girl half-unconscious as a result of the obligatory injection, struggling
faintly, as if dreaming . . . or at least pretending to do so). For from that
moment on, I found it strange that she should react to her abduction
with such insouciance or such sangfroid.

Doctor Juan (Juan Ramirez, whom we always call by what is in
fact his given name, but pronounced in the French way), who possessed

sliver sharp as a little dagger. The girl, who is carrying a
folded cloak or cape over one arm, assumes a distressed
expression, her lips parted in confusion, her eyelids lowered
toward the sudden chaos on the floor. She says: "I was bringing you a glass of bubbly. . . . It fell out of my hands, I don't

---

a huge and convenient, though fake, Red Cross ambulance, was on the
mission, as usual, to oversee the psychological or medical aspects of the
operation. At the checkpoint (the bridge over the Spree that becomes
the Warschauerstrasse), he presented with great assurance an intern-
ment order to a psychiatric hospital in Lichtenberg which was part of
the *Narodnyĭ komissariat.* The man on duty, impressed by Doctor Juan's
Lenin goatee and his steel-rimmed glasses, as well as by the many official
stamps on the document, gave a quick routine glance at our young captive, whom two Serbs, dressed up as interns, were holding in their manly
grip, with no great difficulty, I might add. All these men showed Soviet
passes in good order. The girl had decided to smile, with a lost expression that fit the scenario perfectly. But here too there was some occasion for surprise — that she took no advantage of the police check in order
to call for help, especially since, as I learned subsequently, she speaks
German very well and manages quite handsomely in Russian. Moreover Doctor Juan had made it clear to us that a little syringe of some
harmless sedative could not have reduced her consciousness of the external world and of the imminent dangers threatening her to that degree.

Once past the military post, our intrepid captive emerged from
her momentary lethargy, again struggling to see something through the
filthy windows, doubtless hoping to recognize, in the almost non-
existent municipal lighting, which streets the vehicle was taking. In
short, she was sabotaging my plan of operations. What I wanted above
all was to scare her to death. And she, on the contrary, seemed to be
having fun, becoming, thanks to us, the heroine of a grown-up comic
strip. And whenever she made efforts to escape or suddenly yielded to
panic, this always occurred in the absence of outside witnesses and gave

know how it happened. . . ." Then raising her eyes, she immediately recovers her tone of assurance: "But what have you been doing here for an hour, still in your pajamas and standing in front of that silly picture? I've had time to drink a glass with some friends who are downstairs with my mother,

---

rise to the stereotypical audacities of a theatrical tomboy enjoying her theatrical situation.

Once she was in our lair—a series of workshops still full of archaic machines which might have served for work on fresh pelts: stretching, depilating, and branding with hot irons, but also for the flaying of precious furs, or more simply for their meticulous laceration, or anything else of the same kind—the girl became quite curious about these installations and their problematic use, raising or lowering her eyes toward the stirrups, winches, and pulleys, the big steel chains dangling terrifying hooks, a carpet of raised needles, a long table of polished metal with its cylinder of compressed air, giant circular saws with huge sharp-edged teeth. . . . Continuing, during this inspection, to ask preposterous questions which invariably received no answer, she occasionally uttered tiny shrieks of horror, as if we were taking her on a tour of some museum of tortures, and then, suddenly, she would put a hand over her mouth as if bursting into peals of laughter, for no discernible reason, like a schoolgirl on a class trip.

In one huge hall, emptier than the rest, which we used as an office for our professional meetings, and occasionally for more intimate pastimes, she immediately began inspecting the four big portraits on the back wall, which I had made in various colored inks (sepia, black, and bistre): Socrates drinking his hemlock, Don Juan wielding a sword and sporting a huge mustache à la Nietzsche, Job on his dung heap, and a Doctor Faust after Delacroix. Our visitor seemed to have completely forgotten that she had come here, in principle, as a terrified captive at the mercy of her ravishers, and not at all as a tourist. It was therefore necessary to remind her that she would have to appear be-

and to finish my preparations for the night's work. . . . Now I have to leave or I'll be late. . . ."

"The place where you work, is that a sort of dive?"

"See if you can find a better one in Berlin, among the universal ruins left by the disaster! As our proverb says:

---

fore her judges—the doctor and myself—sprawled in our favorite arm-chairs, quite comfortable in spite of their daily increasing dilapidation, their once-black leather faded now under the combined action of damp winters, hard wear, and poor treatment, torn as well in several places, even releasing through a triangular hole under my right hand, which was absently tugging at it, a tuft of blond tow and reddish brown horsehair.

Ten paces in front of us there was also a russet leather divan in somewhat better condition, under a large uncurtained bay, its glass panes suggesting factory windows rather than those of an apartment, crudely daubed with whitewash. Between the vague spirals of this integument appeared the vertical lines of strong prisonlike bars, constituting an outside protective grille. Looking for somewhere to sit down, our inattentive schoolgirl headed toward this divan, but I let her understand with a few harsh words that this was anything but a psychoanalytic session and that she had better, during her interrogation, stand facing us and keep quite still, unless she was given orders to move. She obeyed quite willingly, waiting with a timid smile on her charming lips for our questions, which were some time in coming, not daring to look at us except furtively, glancing from side to side, dancing a little on her impatient feet and not quite knowing what to do with her hands, impressed in spite of everything by our silence, our vague air of menace, and our severe expressions.

To her right (hence to our left), facing the four emblematic personages so dear to the Danish philosopher, the entire wall was taken up by a ground-glass studio window. Some of the long vertical panes must have been broken during the removal of certain machines or by violence of some kind; sheets of translucent paper now covered the

whores and crooks always arrive sooner than priests! It's useless to hide your face. . . . And dangerous!"

"The customers are . . . only Allied soldiers?"

"That depends on the day. There are all kinds of people besides the Allies: third-rate spies, pimps, psychoanalysts,

---

cracked and missing panes. On the other side, the room through which we had come was brightly lit (much more so, in any case, than ours), as though by spotlights, and the figures of our Yugoslav guards were projected on the bright glass screen, paradoxically enlarged whenever they moved away from us toward one of the sources of light, which made them seem on the contrary to be taking giant strides in our direction, becoming titans in a matter of seconds. These fallacious projections kept shifting—disappearing, then looming up again; suddenly intersecting as if the bodies were passing through each other, thereby momentarily acquiring a presence and dimensions as alarming as they were supernatural. The girl, increasingly uncomfortable in the face of our persistent silence and our stares fixed upon her with a coldness all the more disquieting for being so inexpressive, now seemed to me to be ready at last for the anticipated sequence of operations.

I had first spoken to her in German, but since, in her interrogation and commentaries, it was French which she most frequently employed, I decided to continue from now on in the language of Racine. When I told her, in an abrupt and unanswerable tone of voice, to undress, she suddenly raised her head, mouth open, green eyes growing wider as she stared at the doctor and me in turn, as though slightly incredulous. But her pale smile had disappeared. She seemed to realize that we were not joking, that we were accustomed to being obeyed without argument, and that we possessed, it was to be feared, all the necessary means of coercion. She then did as she was told, doubtless thinking that this sort of inspection would be the least of her worries in the situation of being a tempting victim in which she found herself. After hesitating just long enough for us to measure (a subtle detail with a view

avant-garde architects, war criminals, shady businessmen with their lawyers. Io claims you can find everyone you need to start the world over."

"And what's the name of this *cour des miracles*?"

---

to sharpening our pleasure?) the extent of the sacrifice imposed by so exorbitant a demand, she began to take off her clothes very docilely, with charming gestures of feigned modesty, of violated innocence, of martyrdom imposed by the brute strenth of her executioners.

As it was still almost as warm as summer in those early autumn days, even in the evening, the girl was not wearing much in the way of garments. But she removed each item slowly and with the greatest apparent reticence—though doubtless rather proud of what she was revealing to this jury of experts—and in a deliberate progression. When, after this series of obligatory flexions, she finally removed her little white panties, she abandoned herself to our inquiring stares and, determining to conceal her shame rather than her delicate private parts, raised her arms to her face in order to conceal it behind her hands, palms open and fingers spread, between which I could see her eyes glistening. Then we made her slowly turn around several times in order to inspect her body from all sides, and from all sides it was a very pretty sight, a statuette shaped just like a ravishing doll-child bursting into bloom.

The doctor complimented her on her appearance, listing aloud—with the obvious intention of increasing the perturbation of so obedient a subject—the remarkable quality of the charms thus exposed, insisting on the elegant slenderness of her waist, the curve of her hips, the two dimples in the hollow of her arched loins, the exquisite roundness of her little buttocks, the already-marked development of her young breasts, their aureoles discreet but the nipples already delightfully erect, the delicacy of her navel, and finally the pubis, fleshy and gracefully outlined beneath a golden fleece, still downy though abundant. It should be remarked that Juan Ramirez, a man of about sixty, had once been a specialist in prepubertal disorders. In 1920 he had collaborated with Karl

"You can find as many like it as you want in the whole sector north of Schönberg, from Kreuzburg to the Zoo. The one where I work is called Die Sphinx, which means *la sphinge,* since the word is exclusively feminine in German."

Abraham in founding the Berlin Psychoanalytic Institute. Like Melanie Klein, he was pursuing a teaching analysis with Abraham himself when the latter suddenly and prematurely died. Perhaps under the influence of his already-prestigious colleague, he too had studied precocious infantile aggression, soon specializing in cases of preadolescent girls.

This one, in a hesitant tone of voice, then asks if we are going to rape her. I immediately reassure her: Doctor Juan is merely pursuing certain academic studies of the nude according to objective criteria, but she herself is distinctly too mature for his personal tastes, which do not exceed the stipulations of the strictest pedophilia. As for myself, whose sexual fixations and deepest anatomical fetishes she satisfies—it must be conceded, to the last degree, actually constituting to my dazzled eyes a sort of feminine ideal—I am, in matters of Eros, a champion of gentleness and harmless persuasion. Even when it is a matter of obtaining certain humiliating submissions or of articulating certain amorous practices of an evidently cruel nature, I require the consent of my partner—which is to say, very often, my victim. I hope not to disappoint her too much by such an avowal of altruism. In the exercise of my profession, of course, it is quite a different thing, as she risks discovering very soon, if she does not show enough enthusiasm in her answers to our questions. That will be, she should know, for the sole requirements of our investigation.

"And now," I say, "we shall proceed to the preliminary interrogation. You will raise your hands over your head, for we need to see your eyes when you speak, to determine whether what you say is the sincere truth or outright lies or even half-truths. In order that you have no difficulty preserving this posture, we can make things easier for you." The doctor, who has taken out a pad and pen in order to write down certain points of the testimony, then presses a buzzer which is within

"You speak German?"

"German, English, Italian . . ."

"Which is your favorite?"

A blond lock of hair falling over her mouth, Gigi is content, for an answer, to stick out the pink tip of her tongue

---

reach of his left hand, and three young women immediately appear, dressed in the strict black uniforms probably belonging to a Valkyrian auxiliary corps of the former German army. Wordlessly and with the rapidity of professionals accustomed to working as a team, they seize the little captive with a firmness quite without any unnecessary violence and attach her wrists by leather manacles to two heavy chains that have as if by miracle descended from the ceiling, while her ankles are attached by the same method to two large iron rings suddenly appearing in the floor, about a foot apart.

In this fashion her legs are slightly open, facing us in a rather indecent attitude, but this separation of the feet—which has nothing excessive about it—will make a prolonged standing position more comfortable. Moreover these shackles are not too tight, nor are the chains holding her hands high on either side of the golden head of hair, so that both body and legs can still move, though within rather narrow limits, it goes without saying. Our three female assistants have worked with such natural ease, such precision in their gestures, such good coordination of movements and respective speeds that our young captive has not had time to realize what is happening to her, letting herself be manipulated without offering the slightest resistance. Her tender countenance reveals no more than a mixture of surprise, vague apprehension, and a kind of psychomotor collapse.

Not wanting to afford her the leisure to reflect further on her situation, I immediately begin the interrogation, to which the answers are immediately produced, in an almost mechanical fashion:

"Given name?"

"Geneviève."

and to catch the stray lock between her fleshy lips. Her eyes glisten strangely under the effect of skillful makeup, or else of some drug? What sort of wine had she been drinking just now? Before leaving, she utters a few more rapid sentences: "The old lady who's coming up with your dinner will clean

---

"Usual diminutive?"

"Ginette . . . or Gigi."

"Mother's name?"

"Kastanjevica, K-A-S . . . [She spells the word.]; now given as 'Kast' on her present passport."

"Father's name?"

"Father unknown."

"Date of birth?"

"March 12, 1935."

"Place of birth?"

"Berlin-Kreuzburg."

"Nationality?"

"French."

"Profession?"

"Schoolgirl."

It is apparent that she must have frequently filled out this same questionnaire. For me, on the other hand, this raises certain problems: we are dealing, then, with Io's daughter, whom I believed had remained in France. The erotic object of my present lust would therefore be my half-sister, since fathered, like myself, by the detestable Dany von Brücke. In reality, matters are not so clear-cut. If the presumed father has never been willing to acknowledge the child, nor to enter into a legal marriage with the young mother, his official mistress since two months before the moment of conception, it is because he knew the erotic relations which his unworthy and despised son had first had with the lovely Frenchwoman, relations which had been continued during a rather long transition period. A tyrant in the old style, using first of all a vile *droit*

up the pieces. If you don't know already, the toilets are down the hall: to the right and then left. You can't leave the house: you're still too weak. Besides, the door down to the lower floor is locked."

---

du seigneur, he ended by keeping her for himself alone. Joëlle, without resources, available and on the loose, a little lost in our distant Brandenburg, was under eighteen. She let herself be convinced by the glamorous officer, a handsome man who provided her with material comfort and promised to marry her. Her consent to an apparently advantageous solution was entirely understandable, and I forgave her—her, not him! In any case, considering when this disturbing child was born, she could very likely be my own daughter, her Nordic Aryan coloring inherited from her grandfather—nothing exceptional about that.

I considered the delicious Gigi with new eyes. More excited than bewildered by the turn which her unexpected ravishment was taking, and perhaps moved by a vague desire for vengeance, I resumed the interrogation: "Have you already begun having your periods?" With a mute nod of the head, the girl acknowledged this maturity as if there were something shameful about it. I continued on this interesting path: "Are you still a virgin?" She assented with the same embarrassed nod. Despite her bravado, which was beginning to weaken, she blushed under the cynical indecorum of the investigation: her forehead and cheeks first, then all her tender naked flesh from breast to belly turned bright pink, and she lowered her eyes. . . . After quite a long silence, having requested my approval, Juan stood up to perform on the accused a professional vaginal palpation which, even with the most attentive precautions, provoked in the child a sort of tiny convulsion, if not of suffering at least of rebellion. She struggled a little in her bonds, but unable to close her thighs, she could not escape the medical scrutiny. Juan then returned to his seat and calmly declared: "This girl, child though she is, is an impudent liar."

Our three police assistants were still present, though a little distance away, waiting for us to have further need of them. On a sign

Funny kind of clinic, HR thinks, wondering if he really wants to leave this disturbing house where he seems to be a prisoner. What has happened to his clothes? He opens the door of the big mirrored armoire. In the closet half, there is a

---

from me, one of these women went over to the guilty creature, holding in her right hand a leather whip, its fine lash, flexible though quite firm, fastened to a rigid tip, making it easy to manipulate. I indicated by three extended fingers the degree of punishment deserved. With the skill of a dominatrix, the policewoman immediately applied, on the slightly parted buttocks, three short, sharp strokes at regular intervals. The child reared back each time the whip bit into her flesh, opening her mouth in a spasm of pain, but resisted crying out or letting a moan be heard.

Deeply moved by the little spectacle, I wanted to reward her for her courage. I went over to her, a sympathetic expression masking as much as possible a greedy if not perverse appetite, and I saw, from behind, the charming rump so freshly bruised: three very distinct, intersecting red lines, with not the slightest sign of a tear in the fragile skin, whose satin texture I could now appreciate with the faintest of caresses. Soon, with my other hand, I introduced two, then three fingers into her vulva, which was delightfully moist, inciting me to caress the clitoris with delicacy, attentive deliberation, and entirely paternal kindness, not insisting too much despite the immediate swelling of the tiny button of flesh and the shudders running over her entire pelvis.

Returning to my armchair facing her, I contemplated her lovingly, while her entire body undulated with faint spasms, perhaps in order to modulate the still-painful wounds of the brief punishment. I smiled at her, and she was beginning to return a more uncertain smile when, suddenly, she began crying without making a sound. And that too was altogether charming. I asked her if she knew the famous verse of her great national poet: "*J'aimais jusqu'à ses pleurs que je faisais couler.*"

She murmured through her tears: "Forgive me for lying."

"Did you say anything else that was untrue?"

man's suit on a hanger, but it's clearly not his. Not giving it another thought, he returns to the war mural and to his own image as a soldier, or at least to the image of a man who resembles him despite the bloody bandage masking his eyes,

---

"Yes . . . I'm not in school anymore. I'm a cabaret hostess, in Schönberg."

"What is the name of the place?"

"Die Sphinx."

I was beginning to suspect as much. Her angelic face kept putting me in mind, every few seconds, of a fugitive nocturnal memory. I occasionally frequented the Sphinx (or rather La Sphinge, since the word is feminine in German), and when I penetrated that adolescent sex, a moment ago, with my first and middle fingers, the moist slit of her little madeleine, gowned in its newborn silky fur, spontaneously released the whole process of reminiscence: I had already caressed her beneath her schoolgirl's skirt in that very intimate bar with its favoring shadows, where all the waitresses are compliant, more or less pubescent gamines.

Wouldn't it be necessary, all the same, to make this one submit to the remainder of her ordeal, if only in the guise of a moral alibi justifying her presence in our clutches? I lit a cigar and, after a few puffs of reflection, I said: "And now you will tell us about the hiding place of your supposed though illegitimate sire, *Oberführer* von Brücke." The captive, suddenly overcome with anguish, made a few desperate movements of denial, tossing her curls right and left: "I don't know, monsieur, really I don't. I never saw my so-called father again, once Maman took me back to France, and that was ten years ago."

"Listen carefully: you lied first when you said you were still attending classes; you lied a second time about your pretended virginity, not counting a very incomplete answer when you mentioned a 'father unknown.' So you might well be lying a third time. Therefore we're obliged to torture you a little, or even a good deal, until you tell us every-

and to that Central European version of Gigi leading him by the hand. It is only then that he notices a detail of the trompe l'oeil that had escaped him: the pane which the helpful little girl is touching shows a star-shaped crack, centered at the very

---

thing you know. The burns of a lit cigar are terribly painful, especially when applied to those sensitive and vulnerable regions which you can imagine without much difficulty. . . . The aroma of the blond tobacco will be only the more savory afterward, a little muskier. . . ."

This time my little Baltic mermaid (whose legs were now wide apart) bursts into convulsive and despairing sobs, stammers incoherent supplications, swears she knows nothing about what we're asking her, begs us to have pity on her for the sake of her genteel livelihood. Since I continue puffing away on my Havana (one of the best I've ever smoked) as I watch her struggle and moan, she manages to come up with some information likely—she hopes—to convince us of a goodwill that is, in fact, entirely obvious: "The last time I saw him, I was barely six years old. . . . It was in a very simple apartment in the center city, overlooking the Gendarmenmarkt, a place that doesn't even exist anymore. . . ."

"You see now," I say, "that you know something after all, and that you've lied once more by telling us the contrary."

I leave my armchair with a resolute expression, advancing toward her as she opens her eyes and her mouth very wide, suddenly paralyzed by a fascinating terror. With my forefinger I brush off the cylinder of gray ash from the end of the cigar, which I then puff several times in order to produce the maximum incandescent tip, which I then bring closer to one of the pink aureoles of her stiffened nipples. The imminence of the torture obtains from the child a long wail of fear.

This was the expected outcome. I let the rest of my Havana fall to the floor. Then, with great delicacy and a really infinite tenderness, I embrace my chained victim, murmuring sentimental and quite irrational words of love, but spiced, to avoid too much saccharine, by a few shock-

place where her little fist has just knocked. The sinuous lines that spread from it, in the supposed thickness of the glass, glisten in long ribbons of light like the impalpable metal-plated chaff released by the attacking airplanes so that it will be impossible to locate them by radar.

---

ing details belonging more to the vocabulary of lust, even to a rather crude pornography. Gigi rubs her belly and her breasts against me like a child who has just escaped some terrible danger and takes refuge between protecting arms. Unable to do anything but ask, because of the chains that bind her, she holds out her moist fleshy lips for me to kiss, and indeed returns my kisses with a quite credible passion, though doubtless purposely exaggerated. When my right hand, the one which has almost tortured her breasts, descends down her pelvis to the wide opening between her thighs, I perceive that my young conquest is micturating in tiny spurts which she no longer manages to contain. To encourage her and to reap the fruits of my enterprise, I place my fingers at the very origin of the warm spring, which then gushes forth in long spasmodic jets, my vanquished prey now abandoning herself to her too-long-repressed need, while there rises in a cascade, mingled with tears not yet quite dry, the high clear laughter of a little girl who has just discovered a new and somewhat nasty game. "Now there," the doctor observes, "is persuasion carried to its proper conclusion!"

But at that very moment, a violent sound of broken glass explodes to my left, coming from the ground-glass partition separating us from the next room.

Fourth Day

In Room 3 in the Hôtel des Alliés, HR was rudely awakened by the untimely roar of an American four-engine plane, probably the freight version of the B17 just taking off from the nearby Tempelhof airport. Flights today are of course less numerous than during the airlift, but they remain quite present. Between the double curtains — still in their daytime position, pushed toward the sides — the entire window overlooking the stagnant canal vibrates so alarmingly as the plane passes overhead, at a lower altitude than usual, that every pane seems doomed to explode, the sound of shattered glass falling in fragments onto the floor mingling with the noise of the plane as it gains altitude and disappears. It is broad daylight. The traveler sits on the edge of the bed, happy to have escaped this further incident. His mind is so confused that he is not quite sure where he is.

Standing up with a sort of persistent malaise throughout his entire body, as well as in his cerebral functioning, he sees that his door (facing the window) is wide open. In the doorway stand two motionless persons: the attractive Maria, carrying a heavily laden tray, and, behind her but towering over her, one of the Mahler brothers, probably Franz, judging by the unpleasant voice announcing in a tone of aggressive reproach: "It's the breakfast you ordered for this time, Monsieur Wall." The man, whose stature seems even more inordinate than in the lobby downstairs, immediately vanishes into the shadowy depths of the hallway, where he is obliged to stoop, while the slender waitress, parading her prettiest smile, sets the tray down on a small table near the window which the traveler had not noticed when he took possession of the premises (yesterday? the day before?) and which must also serve as a desk, for before arranging the plates, cup, bread basket, etc., the young woman had moved aside a pile of white sheets (business size, though without heading), as well as a fountain pen apparently awaiting its writer.

HR, in any case, is now certain of one thing: he has recognized his hotel room, and it is here that he has spent the end of a disturbing night. However, though he is conscious of coming in very late, he does not recall having asked to be awakened at any particular time, and he has now omitted having this information repeated more specifically by the disagreeable innkeeper, which might thereby compensate for the lack of a watch in working order. It seems that the notion of time, exact or even approximate, has lost all importance in his eyes, perhaps because his special mission is now suspended, or else merely since he has been lost in contemplation of the war picture decorating the children's room, in the house belonging to the maternal and disturbing Io. Starting, as a matter of fact, from the sort of mental drift produced by that window-opening, walled up with a trompe l'oeil mural, heavy with its missing signification, the preceding night's chain of events leaves a disagreeable impression of incoherence, at once causal and chronological, a succession of episodes which seem to have no other connection than contiguity (which makes it impossible to assign them a definitive place), some of which are tinged with a comforting sensual sweetness, while others rather suggest nightmares, if not an acute hallucinatory fever.

Maria having finished serving the morning meal, HR, who keeps hearing the sentence uttered by the nastier Mahler, instead of demanding an elucidation of the ambiguous "for this time," asks the waitress as she is on the point of leaving, in an elementary but explicit German, about the origin of this name "Wall" that people call him by. Maria gives him a surprised glance and finally says, "*Ein freundliches Diminutiv, Herr Walther!*" an expression which plunges the traveler into a new perplexity. So it would not be the patronymic Wallon which has thus been thus shortened "in a friendly way," but the given name Walther, which has never been his and which figures on no document, authentic or false.

Once the young soubrette has left, making a nice little
bow before closing the door behind her, HR, at loose ends,
nibbles some of the various rolls and biscuits and even
samples the tasteless cheese. He is distracted. After push-
ing aside these inopportune and unwanted foodstuffs, he
replaces the blank sheets of paper in the center of the table,
in front of his chair. And, principally concerned with putting a little order—if such a thing is still possible—in the
discontinuous, shifting, evasive series of nocturnal vicissi-
tudes before they dissolve into a fog of fictive reminiscences,
of specious forgetting, or of aleatory erasure, even of a total
dislocation, the traveler without further delay resumes writing his report, the control of which, he fears, is increasingly
likely to escape him:

After Gigi's departure for her dubious "job," I went
over to the doorway to pick up that crystal dagger formed
out of the broken champagne glass. I considered it closely
for a long moment, from several angles. At once fragile and
cruel, it might eventually serve as a defensive weapon, or
rather as a threat, if I wanted—for instance, to force some
guard (of either sex) to hand over the keys of my prison.
For safekeeping I put the dangerous object on a shelf in the
armoire, where it stood on its intact base beside the delicate
dance slipper covered with sparkling blue sequins, a remote
reflection of the deep water at the foot of the cliffs in the
Baltic Sea.

Then, after a lapse of time difficult to specify, the
chaperone in black arrived, carrying on a little tray something that resembled an American army K ration: a cold

chicken leg, a raw tomato cut into quarters (shiny, quite regular, of a fine chemical red), and a translucent plastic goblet containing a brownish drink which might be a Coca-Cola gone flat. The old lady did not utter a word as she came into the room to set her offering down on my mattress. As she left, still without a word, she noticed the scattered pieces of glass on the floor, which she merely, after darting me an accusatory glance, pushed with her foot toward a corner of the room.

In the absence of any other chair, I ate the tomatoes and the chicken sitting on one of the children's beds, the one with the pillow embroidered with a big gothic M. Though still afraid of being the victim of some drug or poison, I risked taking a sip of the suspicious liquid, which was not nearly so bad than as Coca-Cola. At the second mouthful, I even enjoyed the taste, which was probably alcoholic, and finished by drinking the entire glass. I had never thought of asking my visitor for the time, for her scarcely amenable aspect did not encourage conversation. A rigid jailer, tall and bony in her black dress, she seemed to have emerged from a classical tragedy staged according to our postwar fashions. I don't remember if, stretched out on my mattress again, I drifted off to sleep or not.

A little later Io loomed above me, holding in both hands a white cup and saucer which she was being very careful not to spill—in other words, the repetition of a previous sequence already reported. But this time her black hair spread in shiny waves over her shoulders, and her milky flesh appeared at many points through the gauze and lace of a transparent nightgown suitable for a honeymoon, under which I could discern no other garment and which fell straight from her shoulders to her bare feet. Her arms were bare too, round and firm, their satin skin almost immaterial. The smooth armpits must have been shaved. The pubic bush formed an equilateral triangle, small but distinct, and very dark under the shifting folds of the gown.

"I've brought you a cup of lime-blossom tea," she murmured timidly, as if she were afraid of waking me, though my eyes were wide open, looking up at her as she loomed above me. "It's indispensable at night if you want to sleep without having bad dreams." I immediately thought, of course, of the evening kiss of the vampire mama required by the little boy as a viaticum in order to be able to fall asleep. If my improvised couch had had sheets, she would doubtless have tucked me in before kissing me one last time.

Yet the next image shows her in the same costume and still leaning over me, but kneeling astride me now, her thighs far apart, my cock erect inside her sex, which she moves gently from side to side in slow oscillations, the swaying gestures suddenly becoming more violent, the way the sea caresses the cliffs. . . . Of course, I was not indifferent to the care she was taking with her lovemaking; nonetheless I felt that I was in an inexplicable state of confusion: while feeling intense physical pleasure, I really did not feel I was concerned by what was happening. Whereas in such circumstances I usually take the initiative without paying too much attention to my partner, tonight I was abandoning myself to a precisely contrary situation. I had the impression of being ravished, yet

I didn't find this disagreeable—quite the opposite, only perhaps a little absurd. Lying on my back, my arms inert, I could have come very intensely while remaining, so to speak, absent from myself. I was like a half-sleeping baby whom his mother undresses, lathers, carefully bathes, rinses, rubs dry, powders with talcum which she applies with a downy pink puff, while murmuring sweetly and with a certain authority a reassuring melody whose meaning I don't even try to follow. . . . Upon reflection all this continues to seem absolutely contrary to what I regard as my nature, especially since this maternal lover is much younger than I: she is thirty-two and I am forty-six! What kind of drug—or love potion—was in that fake Coca-Cola of mine?

At another moment (was this before the preceding one? or, on the contrary, just after it?) it is a doctor who is leaning over my docile body. I had been laid flat on my back (from my head to my dangling knees) for an auscultation on one of the two children's beds. The physician was sitting beside me on a kitchen chair (where had it come from?), and it seemed to me I had already seen this man before. His few words even suggested, moreover, that this was not the first visit he had paid me. He had Lenin's goatee and baldness, and slitty eyes behind steel-rimmed glasses. He was taking measurements with various instruments, concerning the heart in particular, and noting his observations on a pad. I realized that it was just as likely that I had never seen him before: perhaps he merely resembled the photograph of a famous spy or war criminal published several times in recent French newspapers. As he left, he said in a tone of unquestionable competence that an analysis would be necessary, but without specifying an analysis of what.

And now it's Io's face that returns. Although this final flash seems to be separate, it must belong to the same lascivious scene: the young woman's body is still swathed in vaporous materials, and she is still straddling me in the same manner. But her loins are arched, her upper body is vertical, even arched backward momentarily. Her raised arms thrash as if she were swimming desperately to escape the flood of mousseline and lace submerging her. Her mouth opens to gasp the air, which is growing rare in this liquid element. Her hair spreads around her face like the rays of a black sun. A long raucous cry dies gradually in her throat. . . .

And now I am alone once more, but I have left the children's room. I am wandering in the hallways looking for the toilet, which I must have already visited at least twice. It seems that the long, nearly dark hallways, with their sudden bifurcations, right-angle turns, and dead ends, have become infinitely more numerous, more complex, more bewildering. I begin to suspect that this situation is not compatible with the external dimensions of the house on the canal. Have I been transported somewhere else without knowing it? I am no longer wearing pajamas: I have hurriedly pulled on some underwear which was in the big armoire, then a white shirt, a sweater, and finally a man's suit that was on a hanger in there. It is a heavy wool suit, comfortable and just my size, as if made to my measurements. None of these things belongs to me, but everything seems put here for my use. I've also taken a white handkerchief on which the letter W was embroidered in one corner, and argyle socks which also seemed meant for me.

After many detours, doublings back, and repetitions, I think I finally recognize what I seem to have a very exact memory of: a good-size room transformed into a bathroom, with a sink, toilets, and a huge enameled cast-iron tub on four lion's feet. The door, which I recall despite the vague light from the hallway being particularly dim right here, opens easily enough; but once pushed wide open it seems to lead into a tiny dark closet of some sort. I grope for the light switch, which in principle should be on the inside wall, to the left. Yet my hand encounters nothing at all like an electric switch or porcelain button next to the jamb. As I advance, in some confusion, over the threshold and my eyes gradually get used to the darkness, I realize that this is no bathroom at all, small or large, nor even any other kind of room: I am at the top of a narrow spiral staircase with stone steps, more like a secret passage than an ordinary service staircase. A faint glow from below provides some light — at a distance I cannot estimate — on the last visible steps of a steep, very dark, and rather alarming descent.

Without being sure where I am going, I venture down, overcoming my apprehensions, following this uncomfortable staircase, where soon I cannot see even my own feet. Lacking a railing, I guide myself by running my left hand along the cold, rough outer wall of the spiral, which is to say, on the side where the steps are a little wider. My progress is impeded by a fear of falling, for I have to explore each successive step with the toe of my shoe to make sure it is not missing. At one moment, the darkness is so complete that I have the sensation of being totally blind. I nonetheless continue going down, but the dangerous exercise lasts much longer than I thought it would. Luckily a pale glow rising from below now replaces that which had come from above, in the hallway. This new dimly lit zone turns out, unfortunately, to be very limited, and soon I must enter a new turn of the screw without seeing where I am putting my feet. It is hard for me to count the number of turns I have made in this fashion, but I finally realize that this strange stone well which penetrates the brick villa from top to bottom leads only to some cellar or crypt a story underground — in other words, two stories lower than the room I started from.

When I finally reach the bottom of this spiral, which seemed interminable, lit only by tiny night-lights much too far apart, I am facing the entrance to a gallery that is no longer lit at all. But on the last step, corresponding to the last dim light, is set a portable torch lamp, the military model used by the American occupation troops; and it works perfectly. The range of its narrow beam of light allows me to see a long, straight subterranean corridor, about a meter and a half wide at most, its vaulted stone ceiling giving every evidence of being quite old. The ground slants steeply and soon vanishes under a sheet of stagnant water extending for some fifteen or twenty meters. Yet a plank walkway on the right side is built high enough for me to cross this pond or puddle without wetting my feet. . . .

And here, between the last bit of duckboard and the wall, three-quarters submerged in the blackish water, lies the body of a man on his back, his limbs outstretched—undoubtedly dead. Sweeping the corpse with the luminous circle of my torch, I examine him for a moment, scarcely surprised by his macabre presence. Then the ground rises again, and walking faster in order to get away sooner rather than later from this compromising figure, I reach a new spiral stairway, this one lacking any lighting at all and its steps made of perforated cast iron. I climb up, making as little noise as possible. It opens into a rusty metal turret which I immediately realize houses the machinery of the ancient drawbridge. As a precaution, I put out my torch and set it down on the lozenge-paved iron roadway before emerging onto the quay, only slightly differentiated from the darkness by a few antiquated lampposts, apparently operating by gas, yet providing enough light to allow a quick crossing of the irregular paving stones.

It is distinctly warmer tonight; I have no trouble doing without my fur-lined jacket or any kind of coat. As was to be expected after my long trip though an underground tunnel partly invaded by water, I am now on the far bank of the dead-end canal, facing the comfortable villa, with its many traps, the doll shop, the nest of double agents, the traffic in human flesh, the prison, the clinic, etc. All the windows of the façade are brightly lit, as if there was a big party going on, though I had seen no sign of such a thing when I left the premises. The central window above the entrance door—the one where I glimpsed Gigi for the first time—is wide open. The others, sporting white mousseline inside the panes, their double curtains open, reveal the fleeting shadows of passing guests, of servants bearing big trays, of couples dancing. . . .

Rather than take the bridge to return to the Hôtel des Alliés, at the other end of the opposite quay, I decide to continue on this side of the stagnant canal and then to cross at the dead end, where the phantom sailboat is rotting. . . . Almost immediately, I hear a man's footsteps on the uneven pavement behind me, heavy yet rapid, characteristic of the low boots worn by the military police. I have no need to turn around to know what this means, and indeed the brief command rings out to proceed no farther — *"Halt!"* — apparently pronounced by a native German speaker. Turning around without excessive haste, I see advancing toward me the usual pair of American MPs, wearing these two big white letters painted on the front of their helmets and holding their machine guns casually trained in my direction. In several strides matching their size, they come to a stop two yards away from me. The one speaking German asks for my papers and if I possess the necessary pass to circulate after curfew. Without answering, I put my right hand in my inside left jacket pocket, with the naturalness of a man sure of finding the object in question. To my astonishment, my fingers encounter a hard flat object I had not noticed when I got dressed in this borrowed suit, and which turns out to be a Berlin *Ausweis*, a stiff rectangle with rounded corners.

Without even glancing at it, I advance a step in order to hand it to the soldier, who inspects it in the intense brilliance of his torch lamp, identical to the one I have just made use of myself; then he shines the blinding light in my face, to compare my features with those on the photograph laminated on the metallic card. I could always tell him that this *Ausweis*, which is not mine, as I shall immediately agree, must have been handed to me by mistake instead of the right one, without my noticing it at a recent checkpoint where there were a lot of people; and I would claim to have discovered the substitution only at this very moment. However, the officer returns my precious document with a friendly, almost embarrassed smile and a brief apology for his mistake: "*Verzeihung, Herr von Brücke!*" Upon which, after a rapid, rather shapeless and quite un-German military salute, he turns on his heels, as does his comrade, to return toward the Landwehrkanal, where they will continue their interrupted patrol.

This time my astonishment is so great that I do not resist the desire to examine this providential identity card in my turn. As soon as the two MPs are out of sight, I hurry on to the next lamppost. In the bluish halo it projects in the immediate vicinity of its cast-iron base, wreathed by stylized ivy, the photograph might in fact represent me quite acceptably. The name of the true owner is: Walther von Brücke, residing at 2 Feldmesserstrasse, in Berlin-Kreuzburg. . . . Sensing some new trap set by the lovely Io and her acolytes, I return to my hotel in great confusion. I no longer remember who opened the door. I was suddenly feeling so queasy that I took off my clothes right away, washed quite summarily, went to bed in a kind of oneiric cloud, and immediately fell into a deep sleep.

Doubtless it was not long afterward that, awakened by a natural need, I went into the bathroom similar to the one I had vainly sought during my nocturnal adventures, of which I then reviewed several brief passages, convinced at first that I had just had a nightmare, a supposition all the more plausible in that I recognized the habitual themes of my recurrent dreams ever since childhood: the undiscoverable toilets during a confusing and complicated search, the descending spiral staircase with missing steps, the underground tunnel invaded by the sea, the river, the sewers . . . and finally the identity check during which I am mistaken for someone else. . . .[12] But upon returning to my couch and its disordered feather bed, I glimpsed in passing certain material proofs of the quite tangible reality of these reminiscences: the heavy wool suit hanging on the back of my chair, the white shirt (embroidered, like the handkerchief, with a gothic W), the bright red socks with black diamonds in the worst possible taste, the heavy walking shoes. . . . In an inside pocket of the jacket, I also noted the presence of the German *Ausweis*. . . . I was so tired that I immediately fell back to sleep, without waiting for the consolation of a maternal kiss. . . .

I had no sooner completed a rapid breakfast, reduced to the minimum by lack of appetite, than Pierre Garin, without knocking, entered my room in his customary offhand manner, determined never to seem surprised by anything at all and always to know more about everything than his interlocutors. After the usual gesture, which resembled an abor-

---

12. Our amateur psychoanalyst here "forgets," of course, the three essential themes organizing the series of episodes he has just related in detail: incest, twinship, and blindness.

tive Fascist salute, he immediately began his monologue, as
if we had parted only a few hours earlier, and without any
special problems: "Maria told me you were awake. So I came
up for a minute, though there's nothing urgent. Only one
piece of news: we were fooled. *Oberst* Dany von Brücke isn't
dead—just a flesh wound in the arm! The gradual collapse
of the body under the killer's bullets—that was all a farce. I
should have suspected as much: the best way to escape pur-
suit, even a possible repetition. . . . But the others are smarter
than we supposed. . . ."

"Smarter than we are, you mean?"

"In a sense, yes . . . although the comparison . . ."

To put a good face on things and not seem too anxious
about the message he wanted to give me, I was clearing up
the disorder which had accumulated on my improvised
desk—I've already pointed out the desk's exiguity, I believe.
While listening to him with a seemingly inattentive ear, I piled
the remains of my breakfast on the tray, which had not yet
been taken away, pushed various small personal objects to
the other end of the desk, and above all, put away the scattered sheets of the interrupted manuscript, but without appearing to attach much importance to that either. Pierre
Garin, I'm afraid, was not fooled. I knew now that he was
not playing the same part as I in our dubious business. It was,
in fact, abnormal—to say the least—that this bird of ill omen
("Sterne" often served him as a nom de plume!) failed to make
the slightest allusion to his brutal dismissal of my services,
nor to the subsequent means used to track me down, nor to
the fact that he didn't ask me a single question about what I

might have been doing for the two (or three?) preceding days. In an indifferent tone of voice, as if to say something relating to the investigation, I asked: "Von Brücke had a son, they say. . . . Does he play a part in your stupendous story?"

"Ah! So Gigi mentioned Walther? No, he has nothing to do with it. He died on the Eastern front, during the last days. . . . Watch out for Gigi and what she tells. She makes up nonsense for the fun of misleading people. . . . That little girl, lovely as she is, has a lie in every bone of her body!"

As a matter of fact, from now on it would be Pierre Garin himself whom I had to watch out for. But what he obviously didn't know was that I had happened to discover, during my nocturnal wanderings through the huge house where I had been, in a matter of speaking, interned, three pornographic drawings signed by this Walther von Brücke, in which Gigi herself was unmistakably represented, despite the indecorous postures, and obviously at more or less the age she is now. I didn't want to mention this in my report, for it hardly struck me as an essential element, except to cast a certain light on this W's sado-erotic impulses. My colleague Sterne's recent observations have changed my mind: here is proof that Walther von Brücke did not die in the war, as Gigi knows on her own account, for all she has to say to the contrary, and it is highly unlikely that Pierre Garin is not aware of the situation; what is his reason for repeating the lie, in this regard, concerning the child?

Yet one narrative difficulty remains, which doubtless counted for something in the deliberate elimination of the whole sequence: the fact that I remain incapable of locating it, if not in space (the room cannot be localized elsewhere than within the labyrinth of second-floor hallways), at least in time. Would it be before or after the doctor's visit? Had I consumed my frugal repast washed down with a suspicious liquor? Was I still in pajamas? Had I already put on my escape outfit? Or else—who knows?—other garments of which I have no memory whatsoever.

As for Gigi, she is completely naked in the three drawings, each of which bears a number indicating the order in which they are to be considered and a title. They are executed on gray drawing paper, format forty by sixty centimeters, in black pencil of a relatively hard lead, blurred with a stump to indicate certain shadows. and heightened with a watercolor wash covering very limited surfaces. The workmanship is very fine in the modeling of the flesh and the facial expression. With regard to many details of the body or of the bonds which fetter it, as well as to the perfectly recognizable features of the model, the precision is almost excessive, whereas other parts are left in a sort of blur, as if due to the uneven lighting or on account of the varying amount of attention the perverse artist has paid to each element of his subject.

In the first image, entitled *Penitence,* the young victim is shown from the front, kneeling on two little round prickly cushions, her thighs held very wide apart by means of leather loops surrounding the leg at the hollow of the calf, and attached by cords to hooks in the floor. Her back is leaning against a stone column to which her left hand is chained at the wrist, just above her head, its golden locks ruffled in an

affecting disorder. With her right hand (the only limb remaining free) Gigi strokes the inside of her vulva, separating its lips with her thumb and ring finger, while her index
and middle fingers penetrate deep beneath the fleece of the
pubis, abundant mucous secretions agglutinating the short
curls there into lovelocks near the opening. The whole pel-
vic basin twists to one side, causing the right hip to project
forward. Some blood of a lovely red-currant shade has
flowed under the knees, pierced with several wounds reopened by her slightest movements. The girl's sensual features express a sort of ecstasy, which might well be a
consequence of suffering but actually evokes something
more like the voluptuous delight of martyrdom.

The second drawing is called *The Stake,* but this does
not refer to the traditional pile of fagots on which witches
were burned alive. The little victim, once again on her
knees but directly on the tiles this time, her thighs virtually spread-eagled by their taut chains, is seen here in a
three-quarter view from behind, her bust leaning forward
and her arms pulled toward the column, where her hands,
tied together at the wrists, are attached to an iron ring at
shoulder height. Beneath her buttocks, facing the specta-
tor (the painter, a smitten lover, a lascivious and refined
torturer, an art critic . . .), gaping wide and emphasized by
the powerfully arched loins, glows a brazier mounted on a
sort of tripod in the form of a candlestick, resembling a perfume brazier, which slowly consumes the soft pubic mound,
the inner thighs, and the whole perineum. Her head is lying
on one side, tipped back, turning toward us a lovely face ago-

nized by the intolerable progress of the fire that is devouring her, while from her fine parted lips escape long moans of pain, varying in strength and extremely exciting.

On the back of the sheet several hurriedly scrawled diagonal pencil lines might be the artist's *dédicace* to his model, more or less obscene and impassioned words of love, or merely of tenderness with slightly cruel inflections. . . . But the nervous script, in cursive gothic letters, makes the inscription largely incomprehensible to a foreigner. I decipher a word here and there, without being altogether sure of reading it correctly — for instance, *meine*, which is merely an acute succession of ten vertical downstrokes, all identical, connected by the faintest oblique upstrokes. The German word, at least if taken out of context, might just as well signify "I have in mind" as "my own," "the one belonging to me." This brief text (it contains only three or four sentences) is signed with the simple abbreviated given name "Wal," with a clearly legible date: "April '49." At the bottom of the drawing itself is written, on the contrary, the whole name "Walther von Brücke."

In the third image, which bears the symbolic title *Redemption*, Gigi has been crucified on a rough-hewn wooden gibbet in the shape of the letter T, its base an upside-down V. Her hands, nailed through their palms at the ends of the upper bar, hold her arms almost horizontal, while her legs are parted along the two diverging lines of the lower chevron, at the bottom of which her feet are nailed on slightly jutting supports. Her head, crowned with wild roses, is tilted slightly forward, leaning to one side to reveal an eye moistened by tears and a moaning mouth. The Roman centurion

in charge of the proper execution of the sentence is apply-
ing himself to tormenting the child's sex, thrusting the tip
of his lance into it, and even more deeply into the tender flesh
surrounding it. From these many wounds in the belly, the
vulva, the groin, and the upper thighs pours a flood of vermilion blood which Joseph of Arimathea has collected in a
nearly full champagne glass.

This same glass is now prominently located on what
seems to be a makeup stand in the bedroom of the willing
model who has thus posed for the representation of her own
torture, beside the portfolio into which I have carefully returned, before closing it, the three sheets of drawing paper.
The contents of the glass have been entirely consumed, but
the crystal itself remains soiled by traces of the bright red
liquid which has dried on the sides and especially in the
bottom of its concavity. The special shape of this glass (distinctly shallower than the ones in which sparkling wines are
usually served, when champagne flutes are not used) immediately allows me to recognize it as belonging to the same
service of Bohemian glass as the object the girl broke on the
threshold of my bedroom.[13] This bedroom, by which I mean

13. It is from this moment—when HR picks up from the floor of
the children's room that odd crystal dagger formed by the main fragment of a broken champagne flute, with which he immediately plans
to arm himself as an offensive weapon of intimidation, in order to flee
the house in which he believes he is being held captive—that the narrative of our psychotic special agent becomes entirely deranged, ne-
cessitating a completely new version, not only corrected in several points
of detail but revised from beginning to end in a more objective fashion:

hers, is in extraordinary disorder, and I am not speaking only
of the various utensils lying together on the long table along
with the creams, greasepaint, and unguents surrounding the
tilted mirror. The whole room is strewn with miscellaneous

Once his light evening meal was finished, HR was visited by our
good Doctor Juan, who was unavoidably convinced that the patient's
condition had become more alarming: a mixture of prostration in a state
of half-consciousness (still awake, though increasingly passive) alternating with periods, brief or otherwise, of excessive mental agitation,
combined with sudden attacks of severe tachycardia and hypertension,
in which was manifest yet again his persecution mania concerning the
elaborate conspiracy against his person, an imprisonment against his will
in which his imaginary enemies were keeping him in order to adminis-
ter compulsory barbiturates, sedatives, and various poisons. Juan
Ramirez is a competent, entirely reliable physician. Though known
chiefly as a psychoanalyst, he is also a general practitioner, though mainly
concerned with cerebral aberrations linked to the sexual function. His
reputation as an obliging abortionist which his jealous colleagues have
fabricated is not, thank God, entirely unjustified—we frequently resort
to his talents in this realm for the girls we employ as models, who on
occasion do more than undress during their posing sessions for amateur painters.

He had no sooner left the improvised bedroom where his patient
was being cared for than Joëlle Kast arrived in her turn, in hopes of dis-
pelling the absurd dark intentions attributed to her by this ungrateful
traveler, whose lodging she had provided out of pure goodness of heart.
Her excuse for coming was to bring him his clothes, which had been
cleaned and pressed—his shoes, his underwear, and his fur-lined jacket—
as well as a cup of Indian tea to which the good-hearted pseudo-widow
attributed virtues much more effective (as both a sedative and a tonic
for the central nervous system!) than those of all other pharmaceutical
potions. Once the Frenchman seemed to have fallen asleep, she left the

objects, ranging from a top hat to a steamer trunk, from a man's bicycle to a big bundle of ropes, from an old-fashioned Victrola to a dressmaker's dummy, from a painter's

---

room, careful to make no noise of any kind before going to bed herself, at the other end of the house. But HR was merely pretending to have fallen into a deep sleep, of which he displayed obvious though fraudulent symptoms: relaxation of his entire body, slack lips, slow and regular breathing. . . . He allowed his hostess ten minutes, to be sure she had had time to return to her bedroom. Then he got up, dressed quickly in the clothes that had been returned to him, removed from the shelf in the mirrored armoire the crystal dagger he had hidden there, and stealthily ventured out into the huge silent house.

Of course he didn't recognize much in this series of vestibules and corridors, more complex than he would have supposed from the way this attractive villa looked from outside. When he had been brought into the former children's room, where a mattress had been placed on the floor for his use, the man was unconscious after a bad fall, upon emerging from an acute fit of erotic hallucinations in the reception room of the living dolls. And when, later on, he had been taken to the toilets of the large pink bathroom where the gentlemen like to bathe the little girls, he seemed to see so little around him that Gigi had had to take him by the hand to lead him to the place as well as back again. HR must then have wandered for sometime looking for a staircase down to the main floor. Everything was deserted, and also very dimly lit at this late hour: a bluish night-light appeared here and there. . . .

And now, emerging from a narrow passageway into the central corridor, he suddenly found himself almost bumping into Violetta, who had taken off her high-heeled shoes in order not to disturb the sleepers. Violetta is one of the adolescent girlfriends of his own daughter to whom J.K. offers lodging, protection, material comfort, psychological support, and patrimonial services (juridical, medical, and financial assistance, etc.). She is a pretty young lady of sixteen, slender and high-

easel to a blind man's white cane . . . and all this junk is
more or less lying about at random, piled up, upside down,
knocked over, as if after a battle or the passage of a hurri-

---

colored, who enjoys a good deal of success among the officers and is,
for the most part, not easily intimidated. But the surprise of finding herself like this, in the lunar obscurity of a dimly lit corridor, confronting
an unknown man with a wild-looking face and an intimidating corpulence made even more massive by his heavy fur-lined jacket, alarmed
her, and she instinctively uttered a little scream.

HR, fearing that the noise would bring the entire household
down upon him, gestured to the girl to keep still, threatening her with
the crystal weapon held against his hip and pointing toward the hem
of her scandalously short skirt. Violetta was wearing the charming
schoolgirl uniform which is de rigueur at the Sphinx, but a more suggestive version that was much more openly provocative than Gigi's:
the blouse, unbuttoned in front almost to her waist, gaped wide on
one side, exposing the roundness of a bare shoulder, while the upper
part of her thighs revealed the satiny flesh between the hem of the
skirt and the elastic garters, embellished with tiny pink-gauze blos-
soms, which secured long black silk stockings, trimmed with lace
above the knees.

Violetta, now terrified at being exposed to a madman's criminal
intentions, gradually retreated toward the wall and soon found herself cornered in a recess between two half-columns by her aggressor,
who was now so close as to be virtually squeezed against her. Hoping to find in this very position her best safeguard in the presence of
an uncontrollable adversary, and having previously relied, in all such
cases, on the acknowledged power of her charms, the intrepid girl
pushed her bust forward to brush up against him, careful to reveal
more of her lovely naked breast in the opening of her blouse, moreover murmuring quite distinctly that if he wanted to rape her standing up, she could remove her little panties right away. . . .

cane. Articles of clothing, intimate garments, unmatched boots or shoes are scattered on the furniture as on the floor, testifying to the careless or violent way in which Gigi treats

---

But the man was asking for something else, which she did not understand: a key to get out of this house, no door of which was ever locked. She failed to realize that the dangerous glass blade still being brandished by this unknown assailant was now touching the base of her pelvis. She gestured as if to put both arms around this unexpected, unforeseeable client, and HR imagined she was trying to escape. Even as he repeated in a hoarse voice, "Give me the key, little whore!" he gradually thrust his crystal stiletto into her flesh, its needle-sharp point disappearing into the tender triangle between her thighs. While the traveler's distorted features became increasingly terrifying, his victim now stood completely motionless, fascinated, mute with terror, gazing at her murderer, both hands raised in front of her open mouth, still clutching the straps of her delicate dancing slippers. As these swayed back and forth, the hundreds of metallic sequins covering their triangular vamp cast innumerable blue flashes in the darkness.

But HR suddenly seemed to become aware of what he was doing. Incredulous, with his free left hand he apprehensively raised the lower edge of the indecently short skirt, immediately revealing the base of the furry little cushion and its illusory protection of white silk, pierced now, where he could plainly see a bright red glistening sheet of fresh blood continuing to well up.

He stared at his right hand with astonishment, as if it were severed from his body and no longer belonged to him. Then, suddenly emerging from his lethargy in a horrified impulse of recoil, he uttered six words under his breath: "Have pity, my God! Have pity!" The invisible glass knife was wrenched out of the already-deep wound by an impulse so extreme and lacerating that Violetta could not repress a long moan of ecstatic pain. But taking advantage of her aggressor's evident disarray, she suddenly pushed him away with all her might and ran screaming

her possessions. A bloodstained pair of white panties lies on
the floor between an imitation-tortoiseshell wide-toothed
comb and a large pair of barber's scissors. What looks like

---

toward the far end of the hallway, abandoning the glittering slippers,
which she had dropped in her overimpetuous gesture of liberation.

Sinking back into a sudden stupor, lost among the labyrinth of repetitions and recollections, HR stared at the slippers where they lay on
the floor at his feet. A drop of blood had fallen from the tip of his lance
onto the white kidskin lining of the left slipper, making a round vermilion
spot, its edges fringed with tiny red spatters. . . . Throughout the entire
household, which had been roused by the screams of the sacrificial victim, doors could be heard slamming, footsteps hurrying down hallways,
alarm bells ringing, as well as the victim's nervous sobbing and the high-
pitched wailing of the other terrified ewe-lambs. . . . It was a tremendous
clamor that gradually swelled, momentarily dominated by the horrified
exclamations of new arrivals, by brief commands and incongruous calls
for help, while harsh beams of light suddenly riddled the darkness.

Despite the impression of being surrounded by pursuers on all
sides, caught in the beams of powerful searchlights trained on him, HR,
collecting himself, had dashed in the direction Violetta had seemed to
come from, and he had in fact immediately found the main staircase.
Clinging to a massive banister so that he could rush down the steps without having to grope for each one, all he noticed as he passed was a small
picture hung at eye level: a romantic landscape representing, on a stormy
night, the ruins of a tower from which two identical men lying in the
grass had just fallen, doubtless struck by lightning. At this very moment,
he missed a step in his haste and found himself at the bottom of the
stairs even sooner than he had expected. In three strides he finally
passed through the main entrance door, which like all the others was
apparently unlocked.

The cool night air allowed him to recover a calmer gait. When he
pushed open the squeaking garden gate, to emerge onto the unevenly

a quite recent bloodstain, still bright red, appears to be from an accidental wound rather than from the girl's period.

---

paved quay, he encountered an American officer who as he passed gave him a stiff little salute, to which HR made no response. The other man then stopped, slowly turning around to get a better look at this rude or absentminded person whom he seemed vaguely to recognize. HR calmly continued on his way, soon turning right to follow the Landwehrkanal toward the Schönberg district. The left pocket of his jacket, though deep and wide, bulged with an elongated shape that was quite abnormal. He thrust his hand in and discovered without much surprise the presence of the blue-sequined dance slipper, which he had unconsciously picked up when he took flight. As for the crystal stiletto, it was now standing on its champagne-flute base, in the center of the hall table, looming like a tower at the top of the main staircase hurriedly descended by the murderer under a stormy sky amid flashes of lightning illuminating the scene amid repeated thunderclaps.

The American officer's testimony is the last of a virtually continuous series permitting us to reconstruct in detail our escaping patient's actions and behavior in the von Brückes' very private villa. HR having vanished into the dead-end alley, the soldier passed through the garden gate in his turn, but in the opposite direction and without hesitation, as a habitué of the doll shop; this was, indeed, Colonel Ralph Johnson, readily identifiable by all of us, as by most of the Western secret services, but better known under the unwarranted appellation of Sir Ralph, which was no more than a friendly allusion to his very British manner. He then ran up the three steps to the door, consulting the large watch he wore on his left wrist. In this fashion we know quite precisely that an hour and twenty minutes passed between that crucial instant and the one at which H.R. reappeared at the Sphinx cabaret (where several of our schoolgirls are employed) — in other words, almost twice the walking time of the girls, for whom this is a customary route: following the canal past the Mehringplatz, then crossing the canal to the left in order to reach the Yorkstrasse.

Probably without libidinous motives, but by a sort of instinct of conservation, as if it were a question of doing away with

---

Our so-called special agent therefore had a certain latitude (twenty-five to thirty minutes) in which to make some detour or other and eventually commit a murder, whether the latter had been plotted in advance or was due to accidental circumstances, even to pure contingency. It may be presumed, in any case, that this neighborhood was familiar to him since he'd initiated his frequent sojourns in the nearby French zone: just the other side of the Tiergarten, which actually constitutes a largely international district (despite its theoretical inclusion the English zone), with its Zoo station constituting the main gateway to the West.

The fugitive, moreover, obviously knew the place where he might hope to find the best refuge during curfew: in the relatively undamaged area to the south of Kleist and Bülow Streets, a sector abounding in entertainment establishments frequented by Allied soldiers and unauthorized socialites bearing the precious pass allowing circulation here at all hours. For he does not seem to have hesitated among the different signs, which, despite their relative discretion, remain easily locatable, many moreover boasting French names — Le Grand Monde, La Cave, Chez la Comtesse de Ségur — but also Wonderland, Die Blaue Villa, The Dream, Das Mädchenpensionat, Die Hölle, etc.

When HR entered the intimate but crowded "concert hall" of the Sphinx, Gigi was standing on the bar performing one of her traditional Berlin numbers in a black corset and top hat. Without interrupting her routine, she made an affectionate sign of welcome with her long white silver-handled dandy's cane, as if they had scheduled a date at the cabaret for that night, which the girl vehemently denies, insisting in fact that she had urged the sick man to stay in his bedroom, given his extremely weak condition (confirmed by Doctor Juan), and above all not to leave the house, all the doors of which, she claimed, would be locked anyway. As usual the little bitch has therefore, in this instance as in countless others, told at least one lie.

the traces of a crime in which I might be implicated, I stuffed
the little piece of stained silk into my deepest pocket.

The evening's entertainment, already nearly over, had passed
without a hitch amid languishing music, the sweet smoke of Camels, the
indirect pink lighting, the gentle warmth of an air-conditioned hell, the
heady perfume of cigars mixed with the muskier scent of the girls, most
of whom were now virtually naked. Couples formed with no more justi-
fication than an apparently chance encounter, a gesture, a glance. Others left the room more or less discreetly, making for separate premises,
comfortable despite their exiguous dimensions, available upstairs as well
as, for special purposes, in the basement.

After drinking several glasses of bourbon, served by a charming
young lady of about thirteen named Louisa, HR, utterly exhausted, fell
asleep in a dark corner of the room.

Early in the morning a military patrol discovered the lifeless body
of *Oberführer* Dany von Brücke in the courtyard of an apartment building partially gutted by bombs, inhabited but in the process of restoration, overlooking Viktoria Park—that is, in the immediate proximity of
the main Tempelhof airport. This time his murderer had not missed. The
two bullets, fired almost at point-blank range into the chest, and found
on the spot, were of the same caliber as the one that had merely wounded
him in the arm three days before, and according to the experts came from
the same automatic pistol, a 9-millimeter Beretta. Next to the corpse was
lying a woman's high-heeled shoe, its vamp covered with metallic blue
sequins. A bright red drop of blood stained the inner lining.

Fifth Day

HR dreams that he wakens with a start in the windowless bedroom of the von Brücke children. The violent sound of breaking glass which has roused him from his imaginary sleep seems to be coming from the mirrored armoire, yet the big mirror is intact. Fearing damages inside the armoire, he gets up to open the heavy door. On the central shelf, at eye level, the crystal dagger (standing previously on its champagne-glass base) has indeed fallen onto the slipper with blue mermaid scales, doubtless overturned by the vibrations of an American four-engine plane flying abnormally low after its takeoff from Tempelhof (into the north wind), which has shaken all the objects in the villa like an earthquake. In its sudden fall, the transparent pointed blade has made a deep wound in the white kidskin lining the delicate slipper, now also lying on its side. The gash bleeds profusely: a thick vermilion liquid flows in spasmodic waves onto the shelf below and on Gigi's intimate garments, which are piled there in disorder. HR, panic-stricken, cannot stop the bleeding. He becomes even more hysterical when the whole house suddenly fills with shrill cries. . . .

I then actually awakened, but in Room 3 of the Hôtel des Alliés. Two chambermaids were arguing noisily in the hallway, just outside my door. I was still in pajamas, lying across the rumpled feather bed, dampened by my perspiration. Once my *Frühstück* had been removed after Pierre Garin's departure, I tried to rest a little on my bed, and, still oppressed by exhaustion after that disturbed night, followed by too little sleep, I had immediately fallen back to sleep. And now the winter daylight was already fading, between the still-open curtains. The chambermaids were upbraiding each other in some dialect with a strong country accent, of which I understood nothing.

I got up with some effort and threw open my door. Maria and her young colleague (obviously a newcomer) immediately brought their altercation to an end. On the hallway floor lay a clear glass carafe broken into three big pieces, the contents of which (apparently red wine) had spread as far as the sill of my bedroom door. Maria, despite her nervousness, sent a smile my way as she tried to make excuses, now using a more classical German, though somewhat simplified for my benefit:

"This little idiot was scared: she thought the plane would crash into the house, and she dropped her tray."

"No I didn't," protested the other girl in a low voice. "She pushed me on purpose to make me lose my balance."

"Enough! Don't bother the guests with your stories. Monsieur Wall, there are two gentlemen waiting for you downstairs; they've been there an hour. They said not to waken you . . . that they had time. . . . They wanted to know if the hotel had another exit!"

"Fine. . . . And is there, as a matter of fact, another door?"

"Of course not! . . . But why? . . . Just the one you know, that opens onto the canal. It's used for hotel deliveries."

Maria seemed to regard this matter of the doors as an example of preposterous curiosity on the part of the visitors. Or else she was pretending to be naïve, knowing quite well what the question meant. Perhaps, excited by the notion of my possible escape, she might even have deliberately hastened my reappearance by provoking that uproar in the hallway. I answered quite calmly that I was on my way downstairs, that I needed no more than the time to get dressed. And I closed my door with a swift gesture, turning the key in the lock as well, a demonstrative gesture which made a faint click, like a shot from a revolver equipped with a silencer.

It was at that moment that I saw my own traveling clothes on the chair where I had put the borrowed suit I was wearing when I returned last night. And on the coat rack at the other end of the room, my vanished jacket was now hanging on its hook. . . . In what circumstances, at what

time, was the substitution made, without my noticing it? Incapable of remembering if my real clothes had already returned to the scene when Pierre Garin had made his swift
visit, I might well not have noticed them after Maria's untimely appearance with my breakfast, since their presence
was so familiar to me. . . . But what disturbed me more was
that there no longer existed the slightest proof of any objective truth about my recent movements. Everything had
vanished: the comfortable tweed suit, the dreadful red and
black argyle socks, the shirt, and the handkerchief embroidered with a gothic W, the tunnel mud on the heavy shoes,
the Berlin *Ausweis* with my photograph (or at least the photograph of a face which strongly resembled mine) but certi-
fying another identity bearing no relation to the various ones
I am in the habit of using, though one in close relation to
my trip.

I then remembered the bloodstained panties, picked up
from the floor for some reason in Gigi's bedroom. Hadn't I
taken them out of the tweed trouser pocket before going to
bed? (In any case I saw myself quickly stuffing them in, after
looking at my double's three erotic drawings, noticing then
that an entire suit is not usually made out of such material.)
Where would I have put them upon returning here? . . . With
some relief I finally discovered them in the bathroom waste-
basket: the room had not been cleaned, luckily, since I hadn't
yet checked out.

Inspecting the panties more closely, I noticed a tiny rip
in the center of the red stain, as though produced by the tip
of a sharp-pointed object. Wasn't there some connection

with the glass stiletto which had just reappeared in my latest nightmare? The anecdotic content of this dream, as is almost always the case, was easily accounted for by elements
of actual experience the night before: while putting the broken champagne glass next to the blue slipper on the crowded
shelf of the big armoire, the fleeting notion of harpooning a
deep-sea fish with this weapon on some underwater fishing
expedition had certainly crossed my mind (O Angelica!). I
carefully put my hunting trophy behind the mirror of the
toilet cabinet, thereby making verifiable the existence of my
nocturnal adventures, careful not to remove the fragile splin-
ter of glass which remained hooked in the frayed silk.

After dressing with no particular haste in order to join
my visitors downstairs, I noticed an unusual bulge in the left
pocket of my jacket on the coat rack. Approaching it with
some circumspection and thrusting in an apprehensive hand,
I found myself in possession of a heavy automatic pistol which
I immediately recognized: if not the very one, it was at least
identical to the Beretta found in the desk drawer of the J.K.
apartment on the Gendarmenmarkt when I arrived in Berlin. Was someone trying to get me to commit suicide? Putting off consideration of this problem till later and not
knowing what to do with this obstinate weapon, I returned
it, for the time being, to where someone had put it before
returning my clothes and proceeded downstairs, leaving my
fur-lined jacket behind, of course.

In the main room of the Café des Alliés, where there
were usually very few people, the two men who wanted to
see me, though without manifesting any impatience to do

so, were easily identifiable: there were no other customers. Sitting at a table close to the street door, in front of almost empty glasses of beer, they looked up at me and one of them pointed (with an almost imperative gesture) at the empty chair evidently prepared for my arrival. I instantly realized from the way they were dressed that these were German police officers in mufti, who moreover, as a preamble, showed me their official cards attesting to their functions and their duty to obtain from me answers that would be prompt, precise, and not dilatory. Although they were anything but loquacious and did not trouble to stand up when I arrived, their gestures and attitudes, as indeed their rare words, manifested considerable politeness and even perhaps a certain kindness, at least apparently. The younger one spoke a clear and correct French without excessive finesse, and I felt honored by this solicitude of the police in my regard, though realizing that I was losing thereby an important means of eluding some embarrassing question or other by feigning not to grasp exact meanings or obvious implications.

I gathered from my glance at their professional cards that the officer who did not employ my own language — whether out of ignorance or calculation — occupied a superior rank in the hierarchy. And he paraded a somewhat absent, bored expression. The other man explained the situation briefly: I was suspected of playing a certain part (to say no more) in the criminal case they had been assigned this morning. Since neither the victim nor any of the potential suspects belonged to the American civilian or military services, it was customary in this zone that an investigation — at the start, anyway—should devolve upon the *Stadtpolizei* of West Berlin. He would therefore read to me, to begin with, the part of the report concerning me. If I had any observations to make, I had the right to interrupt; but it might be preferable, in order not to waste time, that I not take advantage of this latitude and that my personal contributions, possible arguments, or justifying commentaries be grouped—for example, at the end of his preliminary statement. I acquiesced, and he immediately began reading the typed sheets he took out of his thick briefcase:

"Your name is Boris Wallon, born October 1903 in Brest, not the Brest of Byelorussia but a wartime port in Brittany, France. At least it was under this identity that you crossed the Friedrichstrasse checkpoint to enter the western part of our city. However, some thirty hours earlier, you had left the Federal Republic at the frontier post of Bebra with a passport bearing another surname, Robin, and another given name, Henri; moreover it was this latter document that you also presented on the train, during a military check provoked by your strange behavior in the Bitterfeld station. The fact of being in possession of more than one apparently authentic *Reisepass* made out to different patronymics, birthplaces, or professions will not be held against you: this is often the case with French travelers on special missions, and is none of our business. In principle, your movements since entering the Soviet zone at Gerstungen-Eisenach up to your leaving East Berlin for our American zone do not concern us either.

"But it so happens that you spent this past night (of the fourteenth to the fifteenth) on the second floor of a ruined apartment building overlooking the Gendarmenmarkt, facing the precise point on this huge, ruined square where a certain Colonel von Brücke was the victim, at around midnight, of a first criminal attack: two revolver shots, coming from one of the open windows of the apartment building in question, which inflicted only flesh wounds in one arm. An impoverished elderly woman named Else Back lodges here illegally despite the insalubrious nature of the premises, lacking electricity and running water, and she formally recognized you from a selection of photographs shown to her. She testifies that the bullets came from the half-destroyed, uninhabited small apartment located on the same landing as her own. She saw you arrive there at nightfall and leave the premises only after the shots were fired. During her deposition, without the suggestion being made by any other person, she mentioned your fur-lined jacket, surprised that a traveler so well-dressed should be spending the night in this vagrants' rendezvous.

"She saw you leave the next morning carrying your luggage but without the big mustache you were wearing the night before. Although this person evinced in certain of her observations an episodic but evident mental debility, the details she furnished concerning you remain disturbing, especially since, once you had reached Kreuzburg (on foot, by means of the Friedrichstrasse), you asked your way of a young waitress in the beer hall Spartacus, who pointed out to you Feldmesserstrasse, which you were looking for, and where you immediately selected a hotel room—here in fact—some yards from your supposed victim's legal domicile, at present the residence of his former French spouse, Joëlle Kastanjevica. Your steps having been guided by more than chance, the coincidence obviously appears suspicious.

"Now, this same officer in the Wehrmacht special services, one Dany von Brücke, was shot, and this time successfully killed, at one forty-five this morning: two bullets fired in the chest at point-blank range with a nine-millimeter automatic pistol, a weapon identical, according to our experts, to the one which had inflicted upon him, three days previously, only a flesh wound of no importance. The bullets corresponding to the two attacks were recovered on each occasion, which is to say, with regard to the second one, in a construction site overlooking Viktoria Park, hence some thirty-five minutes' walk from here at a regular pace. The precise time of the murder was furnished by a night watchman who heard the explosions and looked at his watch. The two used cartridges of this successful repetition of the attack were lying in the dust in the immediate proximity of the corpse. As for those of the first failed attempt in East Berlin, they were discovered in the apartment indicated by the Back woman, in front of the open window from which she asserts you fired. Despite the fact that this person is half-crazed and sees either sadistic criminals or disguised Israeli spies in every corner, it must be acknowledged that her delirium nonetheless sustains a number of essential points of our scientific and infallible investigation. . . ."

On these complimentary words addressed, in a sense, to himself, the officer looked up and insistently met my eyes. Without showing any perturbation, I smiled at him as if I associated myself with the compliments, or at least was mildly amused by the nature of the text. As a matter of fact, his narrative, which at some moments he read from the typed text but at others doubtless involved a series of free improvisations (his last sentence, for instance, struck me as a personal addition), failed to surprise me: rather it confirmed my suspicions concerning this crime which someone wanted to pin on me. But who, in fact: Pierre Garin? Io? Walther von Brücke? . . . I was therefore readying myself to answer with a certain frankness, though hesitating about what I might reveal to the Berlin police concerning a supposed mission, increasingly obscure, of which I myself was gradually becoming the victim.

But before I could manage to speak, my interlocutor suddenly looked at his superior, who had just stood up. I in my turn glanced at this tall figure, whose face had suddenly changed expression: disinterest tinged with weariness gave way to an acute, almost anxious attention as he stared at something behind me, in the direction of the staircase to the upper floor. The French-speaking subordinate stood up at once and stiffened, he too staring in that direction with the ardor of a bloodhound on a trail as perceptible as it was unexpected.

Without leaving my chair or showing the slightest haste, I too turned my head to see the object of their sudden fascination. Having come to a point facing them without completing her descent, pausing on the last step more or less in darkness, Maria stood beside a uniformed *Schupo* holding in both hands in front of his chest a large flat attaché case which he presented horizontally with respectful vigilance, as if it were an object of great value. And on the lips of the attractive servant could be read the words, German no doubt and articulated with great care, of a mute message she was addressing to my accusers. This young woman, with her naïve airs and graces, must also have belonged to the local information services (like, moreover, most of the domestics in the hotels and pensions of Berlin). As soon as she realized that my eyes were on her, of course, Maria interrupted her gestures, which were immediately transformed into an innocent smile in my direction. The chief inspector gestured to this pair to approach, which they did with a certain eagerness. Maria having removed the two almost empty glasses, the police agent placed his precious burden on our table in order to open it and lift back the lid, continuously observing the precautions reserved for works of art. Inside, carefully set out beside each other and separated by clumps of tissue paper, were seven plastic sachets, each tied by a piece of string to which was attached a tag written in cursive gothic script, illegible to a Frenchman. But I had no difficulty identifying elsewhere in this collection the dance slipper with the blue-sequined vamp, its lining now stained red, the Beretta 9-millimeter automatic pistol, four cartridges which had obviously been fired by the weapon in question, a little naked celluloid flesh-colored doll whose arms had been torn off, the lace-trimmed satin panties which I had supposed hidden from sight in my armoire, a clear glass flask containing an equally colorless liquid as well as a measuring dropper, and the dangerous fragment of the broken champagne flute, its sharp tip still preserving some traces of dried blood.

The officer who had just read me his report asked me, after a silence, if I recognized these objects. I then considered them in detail more carefully, and answered without any signs of disturbance:

"A slipper identical to this one was on a shelf in the armoire, in the room where I slept with Joëlle Kast, but it was not bloodstained and was for the right foot; this is a left slipper. The pistol—which has just been found, I suspect, in my belongings upstairs—was put in a pocket of my jacket while I was asleep; I discovered its suspicious presence myself when I awoke this morning."

"Had you never seen it before? . . . For instance, in the bombed-out apartment overlooking the Gendarmenmarkt?"

"There was, as a matter of fact, an automatic pistol in the table drawer; but if I remember correctly, it was a smaller-caliber model. As for the empty cartridges, I have no idea where they came from. On the other hand, the tortured doll comes right out of a child's dream."

"A dream of yours?"

"Of mine and of countless little boys! As for the crystal stiletto, it seems to be a piece of a champagne flute containing vermilion paint that I saw in Gigi's bedroom—she's Joëlle's daughter—but there were a lot of other things jumbled about there, and in the midst of all that chaos a pair of silk panties stained with menstrual blood. That item, however, cannot be identified with the intimate evidence you are showing me here: it had no lace trimming, and its simple fabric, that of a schoolgirl's garment, had not been pierced at the level of the vulval opening."

"May we know where you happened to get hold of this perforated underwear, discovered just now in your bathroom?"

"I had nothing to do with it. As for the Beretta, the only explanation would be that someone whose identity is unknown to me introduced certain objects into my existence with the probable goal of inculpating me for a crime which I know nothing whatever about."

"And what is the meaning, in your highly unlikely scenario, of this flask containing a substance of which the measuring dropper is still half-full? What kind of liquid might it contain?"

This is, in truth, the only element which means nothing to me among the heteroclite contents of the dispatch case. Examining it anew, I see that the body of the flask, of a vaguely pharmaceutical type, reveals, from certain angles, an inscription in ground glass including the silhouette of an elephant, surmounted by the Greek name of this creature, curiously written in large Cyrillic capitals (hence with a Russian S shaped like the Latin C, in place of the final sigma) and followed underneath, in smaller letters, by the German word *Radierflüssigkeit,* the meaning of which is quite mysterious to me. . . . But an idea occurs to me, recalling Walther von Brücke's artistic activities: *Radierung* means etching. . . . Preferring not to evoke, for the moment, my rival's very compromising drawings, I make another answer of a more evasive character:

"It might be a narcotic or some poison deleterious to
the understanding which has been put drop by drop for
several days in whatever I drink: coffee, beer, wine, Coca-
Cola . . . and even tap water."

"Yes, of course. . . . Your psychosis, or your alibi, of
some machination organized against you by means of various drugs figures, moreover, in the reasons adduced in our
dossier. If you suspect someone in particular, it would be
entirely to your interest to provide us with the name."

Still leaning over the dispatch case, which is wide open
on the table, but suddenly looking up toward the back of
the room (by chance or perhaps because the whispering
from that direction has grown louder?), I notice that Maria
and the older police officer, who've been standing against
the bar while I've been speaking to the officer sitting with
his back to them, are talking animatedly, though being careful not to raise their voices. They seem quite at their ease,
as if they've known each other a long time, though I initially
supposed, because of their serious expressions, that their relations were entirely professional. But then a sudden very tender gesture on the man's part makes me conclude that there
is a much greater intimacy between them, with at the very
least powerful sexual connotations. . . . Unless, having noticed that I'm paying attention to their discussion, which
doubtless concerns me, they merely intend to deceive me.

"Something, in any case," continues my interrogator,
"destroys your hypothesis. On the one hand, this is no
poison, but a correcting fluid, as is stated in capital letters,
though in German, on the flask. This erasing fluid, more-

over, has an altogether remarkable action, which alters nothing on the surface of the most delicate papers. And on the other hand, numerous and distinct fingerprints of your own have been detected on the glass, with no chance of error."

With these words, the officer stands up and closes the dispatch case, whose contents — he believes — prove my culpability. The double locks of the lid click, with the sound of an infallible mechanism which seems to bring our encounter to an end.

"This man," I say then, "who is trying to pin his crime on me is called Walther von Brücke, and he is the victim's son."

"Unfortunately, that son died on May 4, during the last battles in Mecklenburg."

"So all the members of the conspiracy claim. But they are lying, as I can prove. And this collective, premeditated lie discloses, on the contrary, the murderer's identity."

"What would be his motives?"

"A fierce rivalry of an openly Oedipal character. This accursed family is the kingdom of Thebes!"

The officer seems to reflect. At last he makes up his mind to pronounce, slowly and in a voice that has become dreamy, remote, vaguely humorous, the arguments which, from his point of view, clear my supposed criminal:

"In any case, my dear sir, you are in no position to accuse someone on such grounds. . . . Moreover, if you know the whole affair so well, you must know that the son in question, who has in effect survived despite serious damage to his eyes, is today one of our most . . . unavoidable agents,

precisely on account of his past, as well as his present links
with the many shady enterprises, more or less clandestine
societies, and settlings of accounts which flourish in Berlin.
You must know, to end here, that our precious WB (as we
call him) happened, at the very moment of his father's murder, to have undergone a routine check made that very night
by the military police, in the immediate environs of his residence. The coincidence is absolute between the moment of
the shots noted by the construction-site watchman near
Viktoria Park and the moment when WB presented his
Ausweis to the American MPs two kilometers away."

While I compare my own movements with these last
elements of the police investigation, which plunge me back
into intense personal reflections and disturbing reminiscences, the satisfied official gathers up his dispatch case and
heads for his *Schupo* posted at the entrance. . . . Halfway
there, though, he turns back toward me to deliver an additional blow, still in the same affable tone.

"We also have in our possession an old French identity card on which your name, given name, and birthplace
have been cleverly falsified—Brest-Sainpierre substituted
for Berlin-Kreuzburg, and Mathias V. Franck appearing instead of Markus von Brücke. Only the date of birth has been
kept intact: October 6, 1903."

"You cannot be unaware that your Markus, Walther's
twin brother, died in early childhood!"

"Of course I know that, but resurrection appears to be
a hereditary habit in this fabulous family. . . . If you want
to add something to your deposition, don't fail to let me

know. My name is Lorentz, like the providential inventor of 'local time' and certain equations in early relativity theory. . . . Commissioner Lorentz, at your service."

And without waiting for my response, he immediately went out toward the street, followed by the uniformed police agent to whom he returned the inestimable Pandora's dispatch case. At the other end of the café, against the bar, lit now by a yellowish lamp, his colleague and Maria have both vanished. They must have gone into the hotel, since there is no other exit—I was assured—to the street. I remained alone for a while in the abandoned room, where it was getting darker by the moment, bewildered by that doubly false identity card which could be nothing but an absurd invention of my enemies, whose leering pack was dangerously close on my heels.

Outside it was already night, or almost, and the clumsily paved quays seemed entirely deserted on both banks. The disjoined stones gleamed faintly, moistened by the evening mist, which accentuated their unevenness. At the end of the stagnant canal, facing me, the childhood memory was still in place, motionless and stubborn, threatening perhaps, or else merely despairing. An archaic lamppost, directly overhead, its glow blued by the nascent fog in a carefully calculated theatrical halo, illuminated the rotting wood skeleton of the phantom sailboat, eternally shipwrecked. . . .

Mama remained where she stood without making a single movement now, planted like a statue in front of the blue-green water. And I clung to her inert hand, wondering what we were going to do now. . . . I tugged on her arm

a little harder to wake her up. With a sort of exhausted res-
ignation, she said: "Come on, Marco, we're leaving . . . since
the house is closed. We must be at the North station in an
hour at the latest. But first I have to go and collect our
bags. . . ." And then, instead of making some gesture to leave
these dreadful and desolate premises which would have
nothing to do with us, she began crying gently, noiselessly.
I didn't understand why, but I too stopped moving. It was
as if both of us were dead, without realizing it.

Of course, we missed the train. Overcome by fatigue,
we finally collapsed in some anonymous premises, probably
a modest hotel room near the station. Mama said nothing. Our
luggage, heaped on the bare floor, looked as useless as it was
wretched. Above the bed was a large framed image in color,
a mechanical reproduction of a very dark painting, representing a war scene. Two dead men in civilian clothes were lying
against a stone wall, one on his back, the other on his stom-
ach, their limbs grotesquely contorted. They had apparently
just been shot. Four soldiers dragging their muskets, bent
beneath the burden of the task just accomplished (or of
shame), were walking away to the left along a stony road. The
last one was carrying a big lantern, spilling reddish gleams in
the darkness, making the shadows dance in an unreal and lu-
gubrious ballet. That night I slept with Mama.

A light breeze had risen, and the faint lapping of invisible water against the stone wall was audible just below me.
I went back up to room number 3, a prey to new uncertain-
ties and contradictory anxieties. Without any clearly expli-
cable reason, I was returning to my room in secret, working

the door handle with infinite precautions and stepping into the dim space as furtively as a burglar who fears waking the occupant. The room was more or less dark, a vague glow coming from the bathroom, where a fluorescent light was still on, making it possible to move without difficulty. I went immediately to the coat rack on the wall. As I expected, of course, there was no longer a pistol in the pocket of my jacket hanging on its hook. But afterward, having crept along the wall where a bad copy of a Goya was hanging, virtually black in the absence of light, I could see, in a brightly lit area, that the panties with the cute bloodstained ruffles were still resting in the hollow of their hiding place above the sink, behind the mirror, which opened to reveal a cavity in the wall forming a medicine cabinet. On its lower shelf stood a great number of flasks and tubes which did not belong to me. An empty space between two bottles of colored glass revealed the trace of a missing object.

Back in the bedroom, I finally managed to get the switch controlling the big ceiling bulb to work, and dazzled by the sudden illumination, I could not help uttering a cry of surprise: a man was sleeping in my bed. Wakened out of a deep sleep, he immediately sat up, and I saw what I had most dreaded all along: it was the traveler who had usurped my seat in the train, during the stop at Halle. A grin (of surprise, of fright, or of protest) distorted his already asymmetrical features, but I nonetheless recognized him at once. We remained just as we were, facing each other, mute and motionless. It occurred to me that perhaps I was making exactly the same grimace as my double. . . . And from what nightmare, or what paradise, was he abruptly summoned by my appearance?

He was the first to pull himself together, speaking German in a low, slightly raucous voice which—I realized with relief—was not really mine, but a bad imitation. He said: "What are you doing in my room? Who are you? How long have you been here? How did you get in?"

His tone of voice was so natural that I was almost on the point of making some excuse, caught off-guard and knowing myself quite capable of such mistakes: the door was neither locked nor bolted, I had probably mistaken the door, and these rooms were so much alike, all built and furnished on the same model. . . . But the man leaves me no time for explanations, and a sort of nasty smile passes over his mistrustful countenance as he declares, in French this time: "I recognize you—you're Markus! What are you doing here?"

"Are you really Walther von Brücke? And you stay in this hotel?"

"You must know that, since you've come looking for me here!" He begins to laugh, but without gaiety, rather with a sort of scorn, of bitterness, or of an old immemorial hatred suddenly resurfacing: "Markus! That damn Markus, the darling son of our mother who up and abandoned me with a light heart, taking you off to prehistoric Brittany! . . . So you're not dead, drowned as a child in your Breton ocean? Unless you're just a ghost? . . . Yes, I stay in this hotel, very often, right here in room number three; I've been here four days this time . . . or even five. You can check down at the hotel register. . . ."

I have only one idea in my poor head: at all costs I must eliminate the intruder for good. To expel him from this room would not be enough—I must get rid of him forever. One of us two is too many in this story. I take four decisive steps toward my jacket still hanging on its wooden peg. But then I discover that the two side pickets are empty: the pistol isn't there. . . . Where could I have put it? I run a hand over my face, not even knowing who I am anymore, nor where, nor when, nor why. . . .

When I open my eyes and see W, still sitting up in his bed, with the feather bed down around his legs, I see that he is steadying the Beretta in both hands, as in the movies, arms stiffly extended in front of him, the barrel aimed at my chest. Doubtless he had concealed the weapon under his pillow in anticipation of my coming. And perhaps he had been pretending to be asleep.

Articulating his words very clearly, he says: "Yes, I am Walther, and I've been sticking to you like a shadow ever since you got on the train from Eisenach, following behind you or ahead of you depending on where the light comes from. . . . Your friend Pierre Garin has need of me here, an absolute need, for more important business. In return, he's given me this rendezvous with you, Markus known as Ascher known as Boris Wallon known as Mathias Franck . . . Damn you! (his voice suddenly becomes more threatening.) God damn you! You killed Father! You slept with his young wife without even knowing she belongs to me now, and you lusted after her daughter—a child! . . . But today I'm getting rid of you, since you've played your part."

I see his fingers tightening on the trigger. I hear the
deafening sound of the shot, which explodes in my chest. . . .
It doesn't hurt, merely a disturbing effect of devastation. But
I have no arms, no legs, no body. And I feel the deep water
sweeping me away, submerging me, entering my mouth with
a taste of blood, while I begin to lose my footing. . . .[14]

14. There, it's all over.
It was legitimate defense. Once he took the automatic pistol out of
the pocket of his jacket hanging on the wall, I jumped up and threw myself
on him—he wasn't expecting so quick a preventive reaction. I didn't have
too much trouble getting his weapon away from him, and then I took a
step back. . . . But he had had time to take off the safety. . . . The shot
went off of its own accord. . . . Everyone will believe me, of course. His
fresh fingerprints are all over the blue steel. And the Berlin police have
too much need of my services. I could even, as additional proof of my
perilous situation in facing an armed aggressor, have him fire a first clumsy
bullet in the course of our brief struggle . . . which might have hit the
wall behind me, for example, or the door. . . .
It was right then that, turning toward the door to the hallway, I
saw that it was wide open, doubtless since Markus's arrival, he having
forgotten to close it once he was inside. . . . Back in the dark hallway,
where all the night-lights have been turned off, appear the identical faces
of the Mahler twins, motionless and expressionless, as frozen as wax
mannequins and pressed together, one just behind the other, so that
each can observe the scene through that vertical opening, too narrow
for their extreme corpulence. Since the head of the bed is up against
this same interior wall of the room, I couldn't see the door from where
I was. . . . Unfortunately, it's impossible to get rid of these two unexpected witnesses now. . . .
While I ponder, as rapidly as the urgency of the situation requires,
this present configuration of which I have lost control, hastily reviewing

The calm, the gray. And doubtless, soon, the un-
nameable . . . Certainly nothing stirred. But these are not
the heralded shades, nonetheless. Absence, forgetting,
calmly waiting, steeped in a gray medium quite luminous
all the same, like the translucent mists of an imminent

---

several solutions, all inapplicable, I realize that the twin faces are fading
now, gradually retreating. The one on the right is already almost imperceptible, becoming a vague reflection of the other one, paler and slightly
behind. After about a minute, Franz and Joseph Mahler have vanished,
as though dissolved into the darkness. I could almost believe they were
a hallucination, if I didn't distinctly hear their heavy footsteps retreating quite deliberately along the hallway, then down the stairs to the café.

Just what have they seen? When I discovered their twin silhouettes, I had already tossed the weapon back on the sheets. And the bed,
high as it was, must have concealed that part of the floor where Marco's
lifeless body had just fallen. However, I'm almost positive that it wasn't
my shots which alerted those two. They couldn't have got upstairs so
quickly to identify the origin of the shots. So they must have witnessed
the murder after all, without breathing word.

Suddenly I'm overcome by one conviction: it's Pierre Garin himself who betrayed me. He claimed the two brothers were away the whole
evening and till very late that night, detained by an important meeting of
the NKGB in the Soviet zone. Which, of course, had not been on their
schedule—rather, that's when he told them when and where my decisive intervention would occur: at the Hôtel des Alliés, just after the Berlin police had left. Unfortunately, I was helpless against these two-timing
double agents, working half the time for the CIA and therefore enjoying
every possible protection. . . . As for lovely Io, what part could she have
played in this complicated stratagem? All suspicions now seem valid. . . .

I had reached this point in my anxious reckoning when two military interns of the American Hospital appeared in the room, entering

dawn. And solitude, too, would be deceptive. . . . In fact there would be someone, both different and the same, the destroyer and the keeper of order, the narrating presence and the traveler . . . elegant solution to the never-to-be-solved problem: who is speaking here, now? The old words always already spoken repeat themselves, always telling the same old story from age to age, repeated once again, and always new. . . .

---

quite rapidly and decisively. Without a glance or a word to me, as if no living person was there, in a series of very self-assured gestures, they loaded onto a folding stretcher a victim whose limbs had not had time to acquire that inconvenient rigidity characteristic of corpses. Two minutes later I was once again alone, no longer knowing what to do, staring at the things around me as if I would find the key to my problems fastened to some hook or fallen by accident on the floor. Everything looked normal, indifferent; no trace of blood anywhere. I went to close the door, which the silent white-winged archangels had left wide open as they carried out their inanimate prey. . . . Since I was still in pajamas, I decided the best thing to do would be to stretch out on my bed and wait for whatever was going to come next, or a sudden inspiration, or perhaps even to fall back to sleep.

Epilogue

Markus von Brücke, known as Marco, known as "Ascher," the gray man who emerges covered with ashes from his own cold pyre, wakens in the unrelieved whiteness of a modern hospital room. He is lying on his back, head and shoulders raised by a heap of rather stiff pillows. Tubes of glass or transparent rubber, connected to various postoperative machines, deprive his body and his limbs of a great part of their mobility. Everything seems numb, sore even, but not really painful. Gigi, standing close to the bed, observes him with a kindly smile he has never seen before. She says: "Everything's all right, Mister von B, don't worry about a thing."

"Where are we? Why is . . ."

"The American Hospital in Steglitz. Special Treatment Pavilion."

Marco becomes aware of another positive element of his present situation: he can talk without too much difficulty, although in a voice that must be abnormally slow and thick: "And who's responsible for the special treatment?"

"The Mahler brothers, always there when you need them—promptitude, effectiveness, sangfroid, discretion!"

"What was wrong with me, actually?"

"Two bullets, nine-millimeter caliber, in the upper thorax. But too high and too far to the right, because of the gunman's bad position, sitting in a bed with oversensitive springs, accentuating his defective vision caused by an old war wound. That fool Walther's really good for nothing anymore! And so sure of himself—he didn't even imagine his victim would deny him an opportunity for target practice, though it had already been tried by Dany the first night, on the Gendarmenplatz. . . . Still, you were lucky. One projectile was snugly lodged in your left shoulder, the other under the clavicle. Child's play for the numero uno surgeons they've got here. The joint is virtually intact."

"Where did you learn all these details?"

"The doc, of course! . . . He's an habitué of the dear old Sphinx, handsome to boot, and very good with his hands. . . . Not like that bastard Doctor Juan. He'd have finished you off in five seconds. . . ."

"If it's not being indiscreet: who really killed the man you call Dany?"

"You don't expect me to call him Papa! . . . It was Walther, of course, who finally sent the old man *ad patres*. But take it easy: point-blank this time. No way to get his sharpshooter diploma for this one."

"And I trust he's under lock and key, after his new attempt at murder?"

"Walther? Of course not—why in the world? He's been through this before, you know. . . . Besides, family squabbles: we settle such things among ourselves. It's better that way."

Her last sentence was not spoken in the same casual tone that the girl had been parading from the beginning of their conversation. These last words seemed to be whistled through clenched teeth, while a disturbing glow appeared in her green eyes. And it's only now I notice what the child is wearing today: a white orderly coat, buttoned very tight at the waist and short enough to permit a fine view of her impeccably suntanned legs, from the upper thighs to the loose socks. Since she doesn't fail to notice the direction of my glances, Gigi soon recovers her smiling composure, half-affectionate, half-provocative, in order to explain the strange way she's dressed with preposterous arguments: "Nurse's wear is compulsory here, to circulate freely through the clinical services. . . . Do you like it? (She twirls around with a little twist of her hips.) Mind you, this number's also very hot with nothing on underneath, in certain clubs for military R and R. Just like the little beggar girl, the Christian slave, the Oriental odalisque, or the young ballerina in her tutu. Besides, even in this hospital, in the psycho wards, there's a section of affective parthenotherapy: mental health through traffic with prepubescent girls. . . ."

She's lying, obviously, with her habitual effrontery. I change the subject: "And Pierre Garin in all this—what's he up to?"

"Left without any forwarding address. He did in too many folks at once. The Mahlers must have put him out of harm's way. You can count on them: loyalty, devotion, exactitude . . . service and packing included."

"Walther's afraid of them now?"

"Walther brags a lot, but he's actually afraid of everything. He's afraid of Pierre Garin, he's afraid of the two Mahlers—Franz-Josef, as they're called—he's afraid of Commissioner Lorentz, he's afraid of Sir Ralph, he's afraid of Io, he's afraid of his shadow. . . . I think he's even afraid of me."

"Just what are the connections between you two?"

"Very simple: he's my half-brother, as you know. . . . But he claims to be my natural father. . . . And he's my pimp into the bargain. . . . And I hate him! I hate him! I hate him! . . ."

The sudden vehemence of her remarks is paradoxically accompanied by a few dance steps to the rhythm of the last three words, which she repeats with seductive and silly grimaces as she comes close enough to bestow a tiny kiss on my forehead: "Good night, Monsieur von B; don't forget your new name: Marco Faou-Bé—that's the German way of saying it. Be good now and just relax. They're going to take out all those deepwater divers' tubes—you don't need them any more."

She's already halfway to the door when she turns around with a swift pirouette that makes her supple blond locks flutter around her head, and she adds: "Oh! I was forgetting the main thing. I came to tell you you're going to have a visitor, Commissioner Hendrik Lorentz wants to ask you a few more questions. Be nice to him. He's fussy, but he's polite, and he can be useful to you later. Me, I'm only here as a scout, to tell him if you were in a condition to talk to him. Make an effort to remember accurately the things he asks. If you're tempted to invent some detail, or even a whole sequence, avoid contradictions that are too obvious. And above all, no mistakes in grammar: Hendrichou corrects my French solecisms as much as he does the German ones! . . . All right, I can't stay another moment: I have friends to visit in another service."

This flood of words leaves me rather bewildered. But as soon as she's out the door, even before it has closed behind her, another nurse (who may have been waiting in the corridor) replaces her, much more plausible from every point of view: traditional hospital coat descending almost below the calf, collar buttoned up to the neck, coif covering her hair, gestures sharp and precise and reduced to essentials, chilly professional smile. . . . Having checked the level of a colorless liquid, a manometer needle, the proper position of the sling supporting my left arm, she removes most of my umbilical cords and gives me an intravenous injection. It all takes no more than three minutes.

Bursting in the second after this efficient hospital worker's departure, Lorentz excuses himself for having to disturb me once again, sits down at my bedside on a white-lacquered chair, and asks me straight off when I last saw Pierre Garin. I reflect a long while (my brain, like everything else, remains rather numb) before answering him at last, not without several hesitations and scruples: "It was when I woke up in room number three, in the Hôtel des Alliés."

"What day? What time was it?"

"Yesterday, probably. It's hard for me to be absolutely sure. . . . I had come in quite exhausted from the long night spent with Joëlle Kast. The various potions and drugs she had made me drink, in addition to her constantly renewed amorous assaults, left me, by early morning, in a strange state, with a need for sleep bordering on lethargy. I don't know how long I might have slept, especially since I was abruptly wakened out of my slumbers several times: by a big plane flying too low; by another client who had come in the wrong door; by Pierre Garin, though he had nothing special to tell me; by sweet Maria bringing me an untimely breakfast; by the more affable of the Mahler brothers, who was worried about my excessive fatigue. . . . As a matter of fact, in Pierre Garin's case, this must have happened the day before yesterday. . . . He's apparently vanished?"

"Who told you that?"

"I don't know. Gigi probably."

"That would surprise me! In any case he's turned up today, floating in the canal. They fished out his body against a piling of the old drawbridge, at the entrance to the dead-end arm of the canal your window looks out on. Death occurred several hours ago, and it can't have been an accidental drowning. His back has deep club wounds, delivered before his fall over the bridge parapet."

"And you think Mademoiselle Kast knows about it?"

"I do more than think: she's the one who told us about the presence of a body floating under the surface, just in front of her house. . . . I'm sorry for your personal calm, but now you're under new suspicions—you're the last one to see him alive."

"I didn't leave my room, where I fell back to sleep like a log immediately after he left."

"At least that's what you claim."

"Yes! Categorically!"

"A strange conviction for someone whose memory is so confused he doesn't even remember the exact day. . . ."

"And as for your earlier suspicions regarding me, haven't the Mahler brothers testified in support of my story? We now have proof that Walther von Brücke is a soulless assassin. Everything points to him, psychically speaking, as his father's murderer, and perhaps the unfortunate Pierre Garin's as well, last night."

"My dear Monsieur von B., you're going a little too fast! Franz-Josef made no comment concerning the *Oberführer*'s execution. So nothing has come up to invalidate the charges lodged against you in this matter. Besides, we can hardly forget that you were the author of an attempted sexual crime against the person of Violetta, one of the cute young whores working at the Sphinx and lodging in Madame Kast's vast establishment."

"What attempt was that ? Where? When? I've never even met this woman!"

"Yes you have: twice at least, and specifically at Joëlle Kast's. The first time in the main-floor salon where, by your request, the mistress of the house introduced you to several attractive living dolls in an advanced state of undress. And a second time the following night (that is, the night of the seventeenth to eighteenth) when you attacked the girl (no doubt chosen the night before) at a turn of the upstairs gallery giving access to the private rooms or those at the disposal of gentlemen who happen to require them on the spot. It must have been about one-thirty in the morning. You seemed drunk or drugged, she said, and looked like a crazy man. You demanded a key, a well-known sexual symbol, while you brandished yet another in a threatening hand: that crystal blade which therefore figures among the objects produced in evidence for your case. After viciously attacking the body of your victim, you fled, taking with you as a souvenir one of her slippers, moreover stained with blood. When you passed through the little garden gate, Colonel Ralph Johnson, who happened to pass you, observed your distraught manner. Fifteen minutes later, you were at Viktoria Park. Violetta as well as the American officer have supplied a description—of your face and of your heavy fur-lined cloak—which leaves not the slightest doubt as to the aggressor's identity."

"You know very well, Commissioner, that Walther von Brücke resembles me very closely, and that he could with no difficulty at all have borrowed my jacket while I was involved with the enchantress Io."

"Don't make too much of that absolute resemblance which characterizes real twins. It will turn against you the parricide's motives which you impute to the man whose brother you would be, reinforced in your case by certain incestuous relations with a stepmother who lavishes her favors upon you. . . . And furthermore, why should the prudent Walther have so hideously slashed the precious jewel of an amiable person who was prostituting herself with such talent in the heart of his own establishment?"

"Aren't corporal punishments common cash in the profession?"

"I know your habits, my dear sir, and our police, indeed, are extremely interested in the exactions committed upon prostitutes' bodies, especially when they are those of minors. But what you say would not have taken place so furtively in a corridor, when several torture chambers, Ottoman-style and gothic, are available for this type of ceremony, and consequently completely furnished, in the villa's underground premises. Moreover, although the sexual cruelties endured there by the young inmates are frequently long and intense, it is always with their explicit consent, in exchange for considerable remunerations listed in the regulations codex. Let's say straight off that the pretext of an obligatory punishment for some fault, whether or not preceded by a parody-interrogation and the condemnation of the so-called guilty parties, is merely an agreeable alibi which many gentlemen require as a certain spice giving a particular savor to their favorite pleasure. Lastly, the erotic torments then visited upon the captive obliged, if need be, to endure several days chained in her dungeon, according to the desires of the rich amateur who himself usually performs the series of humiliations and cruelties listed in detail in the sentence (cigar burns in intimate locations, stinging lashes on tender flesh with various whips or rods, steel needles slowly forced into sensitive points, fiery tampons of ether or alcohol in genital orifices, etc.) must never leave lasting scars or the slightest infirmity.

"In the provident Io's establishment, for instance, the good Doctor Juan is there to guarantee the harmlessness of exceptional fantasies involving the greatest risks. As a matter of fact, our special brigade intervenes only on very rare occasions, serious madams knowing that any overly manifest abuse would involve the immediate closing of their establishment. Once, during the blockade, we had to interrupt the commerce of three Yugoslavs who tortured naïve girls and helpless young women until they blindly signed a contract permitting the dishonest tormentors to make them suffer even more cruelly, but quite legally, selling at high prices their lovely bodies exposed on terrifying machines which gradually distended them, twisting them backwards and doubtless dislocating their joints, their delicious terror at the prospect of a dreadful fate, their wild supplications, their charming promises, their voluptuous kisses, their futile tears, and soon their barbarous penetration by phalluses bristling with needles, their screams of pain under the grip of red-hot pincers, their blood jutting up in vermilion spouts, the gradual tearing away of their delicate feminine charms, finally the long spasms and convulsive shudders which spread in successive waves over their entire martyred bodies, followed, always too soon, alas, by their last sighs. The best pieces of their anatomy were subsequently devoured, under the label "*Brochettes de Biche Sauvage*" in specialized restaurants of the Tiergarten.

"Be reassured, my friend, such fraudulent transactions did not last long, for we pursue our métier with vigilance, although with understanding, eros being by nature the privileged domain of frustration, of criminal hallucination, and of excess. It must be admitted that once the disturbing victim is offered to his mercy on some cross or scaffold in a convenient and uncomfortable posture by means of carefully fastened cords, chains, leather bonds, and bracelets carefully adjusted to facilitate the many tortures planned, as well as the ultimate violations, the aesthete, intoxicated by the excitation of the sacrifice, may have some difficulty confining his amorous passion within the limits allowed, and still more if the seductive captive convincingly performs the comedy of abandonment, of martyrdom, and of ecstasy. Ultimately, if the condemnable excesses remain infrequent in spite of everything, it is because true connoisseurs especially appreciate those complaisant little victims who apply themselves to writhing with some grace in their bonds and moaning in a pathetic fashion under the tormentor's instruments, with quivering loins, breasts palpitating with swifter exhalations, then head and neck suddenly thrown back in a delectable appeal for immolation, while the swollen lips part wider in a harmonious gasp and the wide eyes spin in a ravishing swoon. . . . Our Violetta, whom you half disemboweled, was one of our most celebrated performers. Men came great distances to see her body distended in a dream of shapely contours, a trickle of blood flow over her pearly flesh, her angelic countenance flinch and collapse. She worked with such ardor that with a little skill a man could make her come at some length between two paroxysms of a suffering which could scarcely be faked."

Can this reasonable-looking man be completely mad? Or is he merely setting a trap for me? In agonizing doubt, and in the attempt to find out more, I cautiously venture into his terrain, evidently jeopardized by the adjectives of a repertoire all too familiar, even to nonspecialists.

"I am being accused, then, of maliciously spoiling one of your prettiest toys?"

"If you like . . . But to tell the truth, we have many others. And we need not worry about their replacement, given the abundance of candidates. Your dear Gigi, for instance, despite her extreme youth and an evident lack of experience, which moreover has a charm of its own, already shows in this rather special realm an astonishing and precocious vocation. Unfortunately she has a difficult character—difficult, moody, unpredictable. She would have to submit to a certain amount of discipline in one of our schools for slaves of the bed; but she rejects any such thing with a laugh. The technical and affective training of apprentice hetairas is nonetheless an essential task for our vice squads, if we want to rehabilitate their profession."

Our commissioner of erotic excesses speaks in a calm and measured tone of voice, convinced though often a bit dreamy, which increasingly seems to distract him from his investigation and to defog him in the mists of his own psyche. Might eros also be the privileged site of eternal reexamination and ineffable repetition, ever ready to rise again? Is it my task to reprimand this functionary implicated in his work in an all-too-personal fashion?

"If you really think I am a murderer conjoined with a madman incapable of controlling his sadistic impulses, why don't you go ahead and arrest me without further delay?"

Lorentz leans back in his chair to gaze at me with astonishment, as if he suddenly were discovering my presence, seeming to emerge from his distraction to come back down to earth, though without abandoning his amiably conversational tone: "My dear Marco, I shouldn't advise any such thing. Our prisons are old, and dramatically lacking in comfort, especially in winter. Be patient at least until spring. . . . And then, I wouldn't want to displease our lovely Io too much—she performs so many services for us."

"Do you also take part in her . . . industry?"

"*Doceo puellas grammaticam,*" the commissioner answers with a smile of complicity. "The rule of the double accusative of our studious youth! To begin by teaching them grammar and the use of a pertinent vocabulary seems to me the best method for the training of adolescent girls, particularly if they seek to perform in circles having some cultural concerns."

"With the aid of carnal cruelties, in order to punish defective terminologies and faulty constructions?"

"Of course! The rod played an essential part in Greco-Roman education. But just think: double accusative, double pain, ha-ha! Barbarisms in discourse always go hand in hand with errors in behavior in the culture of pleasure. To the precise rosy stripes of a supple lash it is therefore necessary, in order to prepare the schoolgirls selected for the plastic constraints of the métier they have chosen, to add the piquancy of a deliberately sensual posture against some column supplied with constraining rings and propitious chains, or on the narrow shelf of a scaffold. . . . Sensuous for the master, of course, but sensual for the schoolgirl!"

As is frequently the case in a properly understood police institution, Lorentz seems to live in perfect harmony with the more or less reprehensible activities of a sector he jealously supervises. I must further acknowledge that he speaks a much richer French than I had first thought in the café of the Hôtel des Alliés, since he ventures into elaborate linguistic tricks and games, including a Latin quotation. . . . A new problem occurs to me, this time concerning the service I myself belong or at least once belonged to: "Tell me, Commissioner: Was Pierre Garin, who is apparently closely linked to Madame and Mademoiselle Kast, also a member of this libertine organization?"

"It appears that Pierre Garin was everywhere, certainly here in our West Berlin, that turntable of all the vices, immoral traffic, and corrupt markets. Isn't it precisely this which has doomed our friend? He betrayed too many people at once. In this regard, I can tell you a curious story, still unexplained. . . . We've already possessed, for two days now, a first corpse of Pierre Garin, whereas he was paying you a visit in perfect health during the afternoon. Moreover we realized soon enough that the disfigured body, discovered in a pool of stagnant water at the lowest point of the long subterranean tunnel which, passing under the stagnant arm of the canal, allows one to emerge from the villa Kast on the opposite bank, was not really that of your unfortunate colleague, although there has been found in his inside jacket pocket a French passport made out to one Gary P. Sterne, born in Wichita, Kansas, which is the most current of his many pseudonymous identities. The only hypothesis still plausible, and certainly the most rational, would be that he was trying to disappear. Doubtless regarding himself in danger, he imagined that the best means of escaping the assassins who pursued him for some motive or other was to pass himself off as already dead. Thirty to forty hours later, someone stabbed him from behind before letting his body fall into the canal, still in the immediate environs of your hotel."

"And you are convinced that it was I?"

"No, absolutely not! I advanced this supposition on an off-chance, in order to see, from your reaction, if you had something to tell us on a subject still in its preliminary stages, in narrative subinfeudation . . . a period quite enthralling for us."

"You're following a lead?"

"Of course—actually, several. Things are moving fast, in many directions."

"And as for the murder of old von Brücke?"

"That's a different matter. Pierre Garin and Walther immediately accused you by name. The latter even asserts that he fired at you in order to avenge his father's death."

"And do you take him at his word?"

"His entire story holds together quite coherently: chronology, the various times of your movements through the city, additional testimonies, not to mention the quite convincing motives which impelled you to parricide. In your place, I should have done the same thing."

"Except that I am not the *Oberführer*'s son. That he was a Nazi, that he abandoned his very young wife because she was half Jewish, that he showed excessive zeal in the Ukraine does not concern me as family business."

"You're wrong, my dear fellow, to persist in this dead-end path, especially with your murky past, your unknown supposed father, your childhood tossed back and forth between Finistère and Prussia, your defective memory. . . ."

"While your Walther is clarity itself, without incriminating circumstances and entirely above suspicion. Have you seen his sado-pornographic drawings and paintings?"

"Of course I have! Everyone has. You can even buy some fine lithographic reproductions of them in a specialized bookstore in the Zoo-Bahnhof. During the downfall of the Reich, one makes one's living as best one can, and Walther has now acquired the status of an artist."

It was at this moment that the stiff nurse in a starched white uniform came back into my room without knocking, presenting me with a little transparent plastic bag in which, she announced in a dry, limpid German, were the two bullets extracted by the surgeon, who was offering them to me as a souvenir. Lorentz held out his hand to take the bag before I could do so, and examined it with a look of surprise. His verdict was prompt: "These are not nine-millimeters, but seven-sixty-fives. Which changes everything."

Jumping up from his chair, he followed the nurse out of the room without a word, taking the disputed bullets with him. I therefore had no clue as to whether the change in question had any relation to me. I was then entitled to an insipid meal, without anything of a cheering nature to drink. Outside, night was already falling, made livid and uncertain by the effect of a very thick fog. No lamp, however, was turned on, neither inside nor outside. . . . The calm, the gray . . . I lost no time in falling back to sleep.

Several hours later (how many I don't know), Gigi returned. I hadn't seen her come in. When I opened my eyes, awakened perhaps by the little sounds of her presence, she was standing in front of my bed. There was something abnormally exalted on her childish face and in her gestures; but this had nothing to do with joyous excitement, or with an excess of exuberance; it was rather a sort of hallucinatory restiveness, such as is produced by certain poisonous plants. She tossed on my blanket a tiny hard, shiny rectangle which I immediately recognized even before I picked it up: it was Walther's *Ausweis*, the one I had used by an unhoped-for stroke of luck as I came out of the macabre tunnel, leaving the doll shop by the cellar exit. And she said very rapidly, with a kind of cruel sneer: "Here! I've brought you this thing. An additional identity card can always come in handy, in your line of work. The photo really looks like you. . . . Walther won't need it anymore. He's dead!"

"He's been killed too?"

"Yes, poisoned."

"Does anyone know who did it?"

"I do—in any case I've heard it from a reliable source."

"And . . . ?"

"Apparently it's me."

The narrative she then began was so complicated, so rapid, and so confused in places that I prefer furnishing here a summary without unnecessary repetitions and digressions and, above all, put in a plausible order. I sum up, then, and I resume: in one of the licentious nightclubs near the Sphinx, known as the Vampir, Walther frequently went to drink a house cocktail made out of the fresh blood of the young barmaids dressed in attractively lacerated vaporous blouses and serving the gentlemen drinks and certain other pleasures. That evening Gigi suggested to her master that she might perform for him—but in private—that role he so appreciated in the Vampir, and reproduce the ritual with her own blood. Of course, he accepted enthusiastically. Doctor Juan himself performed the sacrificial *saignée,* in one of the rare crystal champagne flutes still in stock. In addition to some strong alcohol and red pepper, Gigi, alone in her toilet stall, added to the mixture a sizeable dose of prussic acid, giving the resulting drink an incontestable scent of bitter almond, of which Walther was not in the least suspicious. Just touching it to his lips, he declared the thing delicious, and drank off the love potion in a single gulp. He was dead in a few seconds. Juan remained absolutely calm. He circumspectly sniffed the remains of the vermilion liquid which adhered to the sides of the flute and stared insistently at the girl without saying a word. She did not lower her eyes. Then the doctor pronounced his diagnosis: "Cardiac arrest. I'll write you a certificate of 'natural death.'" Gigi replied: "How sad!"

Once I left the American Hospital, I went with her to the island of Rügen for what she called our honeymoon. However, and by mutual agreement, it was with her disturbing mama that my legal marriage would take place upon our return. Gigi considered this solution more prudent, more in accord with her own nature: without a doubt she loved slavery, but as an erotic game, and insisted above all things on her freedom. Had she not just demonstrated as much?

My impulses of tenderness, as of possession, happened to be somewhat limited by my wounds. My left shoulder had to avoid certain movements, and my left arm remained in a sling, out of precaution. We had again taken that same train, to Berlin-Lichtenberg, from which I had disembarked fifteen days earlier, and in the same direction—that is, to the north. There was a large crowd on the station platform. In front of us was standing a motionless, compact group of rather tall, very thin men with long close-fitting black coats and broad-brimmed felt hats, also black, waiting for something, since the train from Halle, Weimar, and Eisenach had already been in the station for some time. Beyond this funereal or religious group, I thought I glimpsed Pierre Garin.

But his face had changed slightly. A new beard, which might have been at least eight days old, covered his cheeks and chin with a vague shadowy mask. And dark glasses hid his eyes. With a discreet movement of my head, I indicated this ghost to my little fiancée, who after a quick glance in his direction confirmed without the slightest emotion that it was indeed he, informing me furthermore that the luxurious overcoat he was wearing had belonged to Walther. It was Joëlle who had told Pierre Garin to take what he liked from the dear departed's wardrobe.

This made me feel, strangely enough, that he had stolen my own clothes. I moved my free hand to my inside jacket pocket, where the stiff *Ausweis* was in its accustomed place. Doctor Juan had, at our request, made out the death certificate in the name of Marco von Brücke. Lorentz readily gave his consent. I liked the idea of my new life, many aspects of which fit me like a glove. A sharp pain in my left eye reminded me of the battles on the Eastern front, in which I had been involved only by proxy. Once we had arrived in Sassnitz, I would have to buy dark glasses to protect my damaged eyes from the winter sun on the sparkling white cliffs.